A BEAUTY BETRAYED

Impulsively Zela then jumped to her feet and threw herself against him.

"Tell me what is wrong, Papa, and, however bad it is, let me try to help you, if only by listening."

It passed through her mind that nothing could ever be worse than when they had lost her mother. They had cried together because nothing they could say or do would bring her back.

But Zela thought that it would be a great mistake to mention her mother at this particular moment.

She therefore persisted,

"Do come and sit down on the sofa by me, Papa. However bad it is, we will fight it together."

She drew her father to the sofa and, as he sat down beside her, he hugged her.

"I love you, Zela," he sighed. "No man could have a better daughter and what I have done will unfortunately affect you as well as me."

Zela drew in her breath.

"What have you done, Papa?"

With the greatest difficulty the Earl then managed to blurt out,

"I have lost a great deal of money, more than we can possibly afford."

THE BARBARA CARTLAND
PINK COLLECTION

Titles in this series

1. The Cross Of Love
2. Love In The Highlands
3. Love Finds The Way
4. The Castle Of Love
5. Love Is Triumphant
6. Stars In The Sky
7. The Ship Of Love
8. A Dangerous Disguise
9. Love Became Theirs
10. Love Drives In
11. Sailing To Love
12. The Star Of Love
13. Music Is The Soul Of Love
14. Love In The East
15. Theirs To Eternity
16. A Paradise On Earth
17. Love Wins In Berlin
18. In Search Of Love
19. Love Rescues Rosanna
20. A Heart In Heaven
21. The House Of Happiness
22. Royalty Defeated By Love
23. The White Witch
24. They Sought Love
25. Love Is The Reason For
    Living
26. They Found Their Way To
    Heaven
27. Learning To Love
28. Journey To Happiness
29. A Kiss In The Desert
30. The Heart Of Love
31. The Richness Of Love
32. For Ever And Ever
33. An Unexpected Love
34. Saved By An Angel
35. Touching The Stars
36. Seeking Love
37. Journey To Love
38. The Importance Of Love
39. Love By The Lake
40. A Dream Come True
41. The King Without A Heart
42. The Waters Of Love
43. Danger To The Duke
44. A Perfect Way To Heaven
45. Follow Your Heart
46. In Hiding
47. Rivals For Love
48. A Kiss From The Heart
49. Lovers In London
50. This Way To Heaven
51. A Princess Prays
52. Mine For Ever
53. The Earl's Revenge
54. Love At The Tower
55. Ruled By Love
56. Love Came From Heaven

57. Love And Apollo
58. The Keys Of Love
59. A Castle Of Dreams
60. A Battle Of Brains
61. A Change Of Hearts
62. It Is Love
63. The Triumph Of Love
64. Wanted – A Royal Wife
65. A Kiss Of Love
66. To Heaven With Love
67. Pray For Love
68. The Marquis Is Trapped
69. Hide And Seek For Love
70. Hiding From Love
71. A Teacher Of Love
72. Money Or Love
73. The Revelation Is Love
74. The Tree Of Love
75. The Magnificent Marquis
76. The Castle
77. The Gates Of Paradise
78. A Lucky Star
79. A Heaven On Earth
80. The Healing Hand
81. A Virgin Bride
82. The Trail To Love
83. A Royal Love Match
84. A Steeplechase For Love
85. Love At Last
86. Search For A Wife
87. Secret Love
88. A Miracle Of Love
89. Love And The Clans
90. A Shooting Star
91. The Winning Post Is Love
92. They Touched Heaven
93. The Mountain Of Love
94. The Queen Wins
95. Love And The Gods
96. Joined By Love
97. The Duke Is Deceived
98. A Prayer For Love
99. Love Conquers War
100. A Rose In Jeopardy
101. A Call Of Love
102. A Flight To Heaven
103. She Wanted Love
104. A Heart Finds Love
105. A Sacrifice For Love
106. Love's Dream In Peril
107. Soft, Sweet And Gentle
108. An Archangel Called Ivan
109. A Prisoner In Paris
110. Danger In The Desert
111. Rescued By Love
112. A Road To Romance
113. A Golden Lie
114. A Heart Of Stone

115. The Earl Elopes
116. A Wilder Kind Of Love
117. The Bride Runs Away
118. Beyond The Horizon
119. Crowned By Music
120. Love Solves The Problem
121. Blessing Of The Gods
122. Love By Moonlight
123. Saved By The Duke
124. A Train To Love
125. Wanted – A Bride
126. Double The Love
127. Hiding From The Fortune-
     Hunters
128. The Marquis Is Deceived
129. The Viscount's Revenge
130. Captured By Love
131. An Ocean Of Love
132. A Beauty Betrayed

A BEAUTY BETRAYED

BARBARA CARTLAND

Barbaracartland.com Ltd

THE BARBARA CARTLAND PINK COLLECTION

Dame Barbara Cartland is still regarded as the most prolific bestselling author in the history of the world.

In her lifetime she was frequently in the Guinness Book of Records for writing more books than any other living author.

Her most amazing literary feat was to double her output from 10 books a year to over 20 books a year when she was 77 to meet the huge demand.

She went on writing continuously at this rate for 20 years and wrote her very last book at the age of 97, thus completing an incredible 400 books between the ages of 77 and 97.

Her publishers finally could not keep up with this phenomenal output, so at her death in 2000 she left behind an amazing 160 unpublished manuscripts, something that no other author has ever achieved.

Barbara's son, Ian McCorquodale, together with his daughter Iona, felt that it was their sacred duty to publish all these titles for Barbara's millions of admirers all over the world who so love her wonderful romances.

So in 2004 they started publishing the 160 brand new Barbara Cartlands as *The Barbara Cartland Pink Collection*, as Barbara's favourite colour was always pink – and yet more pink!

The Barbara Cartland Pink Collection is published monthly exclusively by Barbaracartland.com and the books are numbered in sequence from 1 to 160.

Enjoy receiving a brand new Barbara Cartland book each month by taking out an annual subscription to the Pink Collection, or purchase the books individually.

The Pink Collection is available from the Barbara Cartland website www.barbaracartland.com via mail order and through all good bookshops.

In addition Ian and Iona are proud to announce that The Barbara Cartland Pink Collection is now available in ebook format as from Valentine's Day 2011.

For more information, please contact us at:

Barbaracartland.com Ltd.
Camfield Place
Hatfield
Hertfordshire AL9 6JE
United Kingdom

Telephone: +44 (0)1707 642629
Fax: +44 (0)1707 663041
Email: info@barbaracartland.com

THE LATE DAME BARBARA CARTLAND

Barbara Cartland who sadly died in May 2000 at the age of nearly 99 was the world's most famous romantic novelist who wrote 723 books in her lifetime with worldwide sales of over 1 billion copies and her books were translated into 36 different languages.

As well as romantic novels, she wrote historical biographies, 6 autobiographies, theatrical plays, books of advice on life, love, vitamins and cookery. She also found time to be a political speaker and television and radio personality.

She wrote her first book at the age of 21 and this was called *Jigsaw*. It became an immediate bestseller and sold 100,000 copies in hardback and was translated into 6 different languages. She wrote continuously throughout her life, writing bestsellers for an astonishing 76 years. Her books have always been immensely popular in the United States, where in 1976 her current books were at numbers 1 & 2 in the B. Dalton bestsellers list, a feat never achieved before or since by any author.

Barbara Cartland became a legend in her own lifetime and will be best remembered for her wonderful romantic novels, so loved by her millions of readers throughout the world.

Her books will always be treasured for their moral message, her pure and innocent heroines, her good looking and dashing heroes and above all her belief that the power of love is more important than anything else in everyone's life.

"God taught us to love and only with love can we ever find a Heaven on Earth."

Barbara Cartland

CHAPTER ONE
1885

Lady Zela Lang trotted briskly into the stable yard and a groom came running out to hold her horse's head.

"'Ave you 'ad a good ride, my Lady?" he enquired.

"Really lovely, thank you, Armstrong," Lady Zela replied. "It's a marvellous day and I could go on riding for hours."

"'Is Lordship should be back 'ere soon," Armstrong remarked.

"Yes!" Lady Zela said. "And it will be delightful to see him."

Armstrong, who was now leading the horse to the stable, then said,

"I thinks, my Lady, you ought to ask 'im if we can 'ave another 'orse or two. Poor old Robin won't last for much longer."

"I know that," Lady Zela replied.

"What you wants, my Lady," he carried on, "is a good 'unter for the winter and 'is Lordship'll want the same. Those we've got 'ave served us real well, but neither them nor us'll last for ever!"

"That is very true," Lady Zela agreed, "and I will certainly speak to his Lordship."

She walked across the cobbled yard and through the arched door that led to the front of the house.

The sun was shining on the windows and Langdale Hall was looking very beautiful.

It had been in the family since the reign of Charles II and now that the bricks had mellowed over the years it was even more attractive than it must have been then.

Lady Zela loved her home, but since her beloved mother had died she was very much alone.

Nevertheless Zela was exceedingly happy galloping over the fields and tending the somewhat wild garden.

The trouble was, and it was nothing new, that there was not enough money!

It cost money that they did not have to keep it in the way it had been in her grandfather and great-grandfather's time.

Back then the reigning Earl had employed a large number of indoor and outdoor staff.

But today, whatever Zela asked her father to buy or do, he claimed at once that he could not afford it.

At the same time he had taken lately to going to London and she could understand that he found it dull in the country without her mother.

As he was still a very attractive man, he enjoyed being with his friends and making new acquaintances.

London gave him not only his contemporaries, who he found at White's Club, but he was also eagerly sought after by the hostesses who made the Social life of London the most attractive and amusing in Europe.

People who came from Paris always said that they could not compete with London and the Germans were just plain envious.

So it was not surprising that the Prince of Wales enjoyed going to a party or giving one almost every night and then he was able to pursue those who were known as the 'Professional Beauties'.

When His Royal Highness fell in love with Lillie Langtry, she was undoubtedly one of the greatest beauties that England had ever seen.

It then became possible, for the first time in social history, for a gentleman to be able to conduct an *affaire-de-coeur* with a lady of his own class.

Previously there was an enormous division between the Cyprians and Ladies of Quality and it was impossible for the two to ever meet.

But Lillie Langtry had been accepted by Princess Alexandra, the long suffering Princess of Wales.

All the hostesses of Mayfair had then followed her example, while the Prince of Wales had moved from one beauty to another. There were many entries in the Betting Book at White's as to who would be the next!

The Earl of Langdale was an extremely handsome man and he was still exceptionally good-looking when he became a widower at only forty-three.

It was not surprising that a number of women found him most attractive and they pursued him relentlessly.

He had at first, when his adored wife died suddenly for no good reason that any of her doctors could diagnose, remained gloomily in the country.

He was alone except for his daughter, who was still at the age when she was being instructed by Governesses and Tutors.

It was one of his old school friends who had then persuaded him to come to London.

"Do stay with us for a few nights, David," he urged, "and I will show you round."

The Earl took quite a lot of persuading, but finally he accepted his friend's invitation.

When he reached London, he found at once that it was everything he had missed for so long without realising it and a good deal more. In fact he had been so happily married that he had never thought about it.

He went to Whites and found a great number of his school friends in the Club as well as those he had studied with at Oxford University. They had not forgotten him and greeted him with delight.

"Now that you are back in circulation, David," they said, "we will make sure that you enjoy yourself."

They took the Earl from party to party.

He had been in London for barely ten days when he found that he had attracted the attention of one of the most outstanding of the 'Professional Beauties'.

He found that being with her and making love to her helped him forget his unhappiness and despair at losing his very special wife.

His second visit to London, this time staying with another old friend of his who was anxious to entertain him, was also a great success.

It was then that the Earl decided that he must have a *pied-a-terre* of his own in London and he found a small cheap flat in Half Moon Street just off Piccadilly in the heart of Mayfair.

And so his visits to the country grew fewer as the invitations from London hostesses continued to pour in.

He was, however, coming back to his home today.

His daughter, Zela, was determined that he should enjoy himself and she had had a long conversation this morning with the cook.

Mrs. Brunt had been Langdale Hall for thirty years and she was a very good cook when she had all the right ingredients and she had been preparing all week for his Lordship's return.

"I've planned all your father's favourite dishes, my Lady," she said to Zela. "Brunt has brought up a bottle of champagne from the cellar and a fine old brandy that he says were put there when we were fightin' Napoleon."

Zela had laughed.

"I expect it was smuggled," she said. "And I have always been told that, as the very best brandy comes from France, the gentlemen in England drank it during the War against Napoleon as they could only obtain it from the smugglers."

"Well, however we got it," Mrs. Brunt replied, "I knows his Lordship'll really enjoy it."

"I know he will too," Zela said, "and he will be delighted to eat all the dishes you are cooking for him."

She left the kitchen to put flowers in her father's study, as she thought that he would rather sit there than in the drawing room, which would inevitably make him think of her mother because it had been her favourite room.

She had made it very beautiful, just as she had with everything around her, and Zela had heard her father say so often that she was as lovely as she had made the house.

The Countess had died one cold winter's day and no one could do anything to save her. The doctors were helpless and she passed away quietly while everyone who loved her was deeply shocked.

It happened so unexpectedly that it was difficult for her husband and daughter to believe that she had really left them.

At first the Earl was so depressed that Zela could do nothing to cheer him up.

Yet there were still horses to ride and there was still plenty to organise on the estate.

Finally he began to pay attention to the everyday problems that at first he had refused to even recognise.

As soon as he had started going to London, Zela had to admit that he was a different man.

He would tell her about the parties he had been to and the people he had met and he would relate what was being performed at *Drury Lane*.

What Zela enjoyed hearing about most of all was the horses. They were to be seen daily in Rotten Row and her father was lent horses by his many friends.

"I was lent an Arab," he had said the last time that he come home. "It was the best horse I have ever ridden and by far the most impressive."

"I am sure you looked handsome and magnificent on him, Papa," Zela smiled.

Her father had laughed, but what she had said was true. Because he was so handsome, it would have been just impossible for the ladies who attended Rotten Row in their open Victorias not to notice him.

Fortunately the walls in the Earl's study that were not covered with books were not in as bad a state as they were in some of the other rooms.

The whole house needed a great deal of attention and the ceilings were either cracked or discoloured and the walls needed painting or repapering.

And a good many of the diamond-paned windows were broken.

Zela had grown used to the dilapidated state of the house and tried to ignore how much there was to be done everywhere.

Looking at it now she thought that it would be just impossible for her father not to compare it with the houses where he had been staying not only in London but in the country as well.

He had been invited at weekends to parties that had included the Prince of Wales.

The Prince had asked for him because he found him so amusing. He always enjoyed being with him, a man like himself who attracted beautiful women.

'I have done my best to make it look as attractive as possible,' Zela thought as she looked around the study. 'I only wish that we could have the pictures cleaned. Some of the oldest ones are in a really deplorable state.'

Then she remembered what Armstrong had said to her and, of course, her father must have a good horse to ride in the winter.

The horses he already had, although he loved them, would not be able to keep up with the Hunt.

Zela was still in the study when she thought that she heard the sound of wheels outside.

She ran along the passage to the hall and found that she had not been mistaken.

Her father had come home in a post chaise drawn by two horses and, as he climbed out, Zela ran down the steps to fling herself against him.

"You are home, Papa! It's wonderful to see you!"

He kissed his daughter affectionately and said,

"Let me pay this man now and tell him that he can have something to eat before he returns to London."

He took some money from his pocket as he spoke and Zela could not help hoping that he had a great deal more.

The Earl put his arm around Zela's shoulders and they walked up the steps and into the house.

"How are you, my dearest Zela?" he asked. "You are looking very lovely and, seeing how you are dressed, I would suppose that you have been riding this morning?"

"I have, Papa, and I want to talk to you about the horses. But do tell me first what you have been doing in London."

The Earl evaded her question.

After he had washed his hands, they went into the dining room together for a late luncheon.

It was then that Zela realised for the first time that something was wrong.

Her father seemed to be strangely reluctant to talk to her about what he had been doing in London.

Knowing him so well Zela now perceived from the expression in his eyes and the way he spoke that he was worried and upset about something.

He was looking, she felt, exceedingly handsome in the smart clothes he wore in London.

When they had finished luncheon, Brunt put a large glass of Napoleon brandy at her father's side. And then he withdrew into the pantry closing the door behind him.

Zela bent forward and put her hand on her father's.

"What is upsetting you, Papa?" she asked. "I know that something is wrong. Tell me about it, please."

For a moment there was silence.

And then the Earl began,

"It is something I am finding very difficult to relate to you, my dearest."

Zela felt her heart give a little throb.

It flashed through her mind that perhaps her father was going to marry again.

It was an eventuality that she had always feared.

She thought that in his loneliness he might find any woman, whatever she was like, better than having no one to talk to except herself.

Her father rose from the table.

"Let's go to the study," he suggested. "What I have to tell you is for your ears alone."

Zela wondered what it could possibly be, as her father picked up his glass of brandy.

When they entered the study, the arrangements of flowers and the bright afternoon sun streaming in through the windows made the room seem very attractive.

The Earl walked over to the mantelpiece and put his brandy glass on it and then he turned to face his daughter.

Without being told, but because she knew that it was expected of her, Zela sat down in an armchair facing him.

There was a poignant silence and then finally Zela asked,

"Tell me what is worrying you, Papa. You know I love you and, however upsetting it may be, I want to help you if I possibly can."

The Earl gave a flicker of a smile.

"That is exactly what I would expect you to say, my dearest. Unfortunately no one can help me at the moment because for one thing I have no intention of telling anyone but you what has happened."

Zela clasped her fingers together.

"What *has* happened, Papa?" she insisted, feeling even more apprehensive than before luncheon.

She knew by the way her father hesitated that it was painful for him to find the words to answer her.

Impulsively Zela then jumped to her feet and threw herself against him.

"Tell me what is wrong, Papa, and, however bad it is, let me try to help you, if only by listening."

It passed through her mind that nothing could ever be worse than when they had lost her mother. They had cried together because nothing they could say or do would bring her back.

But Zela thought that it would be a great mistake to mention her mother at this particular moment.

She therefore persisted,

"Do come and sit down on the sofa by me, Papa. However awful it is, we will fight it together."

She drew her father to the sofa and, as he sat down beside her, he hugged her.

"I love you, Zela," he sighed. "No man could have a better daughter and what I have done will unfortunately affect you as well as me."

Zela drew in her breath.

"What have you done, Papa?"

With the greatest difficulty the Earl then managed to blurt out,

"I have lost a great deal of money, more than we can possibly afford."

Zela's eyes widened.

"But how, Papa? How could you have done so?"

She was thinking as she spoke that there had never been very much money for them to spend.

And she realised, because her father was actually so popular, that, apart from his small cheap flat, he actually spent very little of his own money when he was in London as he was always being entertained by his friends.

There was another silence and then the Earl said,

"I think you have heard me speak of the Comtesse de Courché."

"Yes, I have, Papa."

She was astute enough to realise what the Comtesse meant to him.

The last time he came home, which was only for a few days, she was aware that her father was spending most of his time with the Comtesse.

Zela had read about her. In *The Court Circular* she was mentioned almost every day as well as in the ladies' magazines.

The Comtesse had only recently come to London, but she was immediately acclaimed as a great beauty and her name was constantly on everyone's lips.

Zela had known by the way her father spoke of her, without him giving any explanation, that he was attracted by the Comtesse and she very obviously meant something in his life.

Zela had been alarmed by her father's depression after her mother's death and she recognised that his new life in London was giving him back his *joie de vivre*.

It was an attribute that he had always had and her mother had thought it was one of the most precious things about him.

"Your father enjoys life," she had said to Zela. "To everything he does and to everything he is interested in he gives a part of himself."

"I know that, Mama," Zela had replied.

"The French call it *joie de vivre*," her mother went on. "To us it is a joy of living that few people are fortunate enough to have."

Zela had understood because she felt in some ways that she was very like her father and this was definitely one of them.

It had, therefore, been an irrepressible relief to see, after he had first visited London, that he was almost his old self again.

She was not the least bit jealous as some daughters might have been and she was very grateful, although she had never met them, to the women who were making her father himself once more.

He did not have to tell her who they were, as she knew at once by the way he mentioned their names, when he referred to them as being at one party or another and looking 'extremely beautiful' or 'particularly attractive'.

There was then a note in his voice, which had been there when he had been talking to her mother.

Zela had often heard him say,

"You are so exquisitely lovely, my darling, that I feel as if you cannot be real. If you are, then how can I be so lucky as to have you in my life?"

When he said something like that to her, her mother would laugh and kiss him.

Zela knew that it was impossible to find two people who were happier with each other. They thought the same about everything and were undoubtedly the other half of each other.

So she had known the very first time that her father had mentioned the Comtesse de Courché that she meant something special to him.

He had brought that note of excitement back into his voice which meant that he was attracted by her.

And Zela was also quite certain that the Comtesse was attracted by him.

The Earl did not say anything, but letters would arrive at Langdale Hall and the writing on the envelopes was not only that of a woman but, as Zela quickly noticed, she was French rather than English.

What had often passed through her mind was that maybe the women her father was attracted to might expect him to give them expensive presents.

She had always understood that Cyprians expected gifts of precious jewels and money, while a Lady could only receive flowers, scent or a pretty fan.

Even these could be expensive and were luxuries that her father could not afford.

Now, as the Earl broke the long silence, she held her breath.

"It might seem to you incredible that I should be so stupid, so utterly and completely foolish," he was saying. "But it seemed to me to be the chance of a lifetime and if, as I was assured that everything would happen the way it should, my money would not only have trebled but would be ten or twenty times more than the sum I had originally invested."

Zela looked at her father in astonishment.

"You invested money, Papa, but how could you do that when we have so little in the bank?"

"I can hardly tell you how idiotic I have been," the Earl answered, "but I was told that I would be a fool to refuse what seemed to me at any rate to be a gift from the Gods."

Zela slipped her hand into his.

"Start right at the beginning, Papa," she said softly, "and tell me exactly what has happened."

The Earl's fingers closed over hers as he lay back on the sofa.

"I was with the Comtesse de Courché," he began, "when she was opening her letters. She received one that made her give a cry of surprise and delight.

"'What is it?' I asked her.

"'Something amazing and fantastic has happened,' she replied, 'and, although I thought that it was an outside chance, I have made a great deal of money'.

"I quite naturally asked her to tell me all about it," the Earl said, "and she told me that she had a friend who was bringing special products into France from one of the Eastern countries."

"What sort of products?" Zela enquired.

"The most important was oil," the Earl answered. "As you know with trains, ships and, of course, factories, oil in the last four years has become an essential part of our daily lives."

"Of course I understand that," Zela said, "do go on, Papa."

"The Comtesse told me that her friend was working with one Eastern country which has a lot of oil and a great many other materials that are needed in the West."

"Surely the Government should be buying them?" Zela queried.

"I felt you would think of that," her father replied. "You are a clever girl and thank Heavens, unlike some women, you have a very intelligent brain."

"But I take after you, but do carry on, Papa."

"What it amounted to," her father said slowly, "was that the Ruler of this country, like all Easterners, wanted to have his personal share of whatever was sold."

Zela stared at the Earl.

"Do you mean secretly?" she asked.

"Yes, secretly," he answered. "It is quite common in the East. Everyone takes a rake-off sooner or later."

He paused for a moment before continuing,

"But in this case the Ruler himself was arranging that all these products should leave his country not through the usual channels, but in a secret way that would benefit him."

"I think I understand," Zela said. "But, of course, what he is doing is wrong."

"It is certainly wrong for him, but, as we are only the participants, we could not be blamed for taking what we were offered and not ask too many inquisitive questions as to how we obtained it."

"And the Comtesse herself has benefitted greatly by this new arrangement?" Zela asked.

"She has gained, she told me, very considerably," the Earl replied. "And, because she is fond of me, she has offered me a chance to make a fortune too."

He did not say more until Zela quizzed him,

"Then somehow, Papa, you found the money. But what did you buy?"

"It was not quite as easy as that," he said. "What was coming into France through a friend of the Comtesse was oil and other products that only the East could supply, such as hand-woven carpets, jewels and quite a number of other luxuries that are not obtainable in the West."

Zela did not speak and after a moment he added,

"Of course the most important was the oil because, at the moment, in England we have no oil of our own and the Comtesse tells me that it is the same in France."

"So what did you do?" Zela asked, feeling that she already knew the answer.

"I went to my bank," the Earl said, "and by putting up as a guarantee, the house, the estate, in fact everything we possess, I borrowed the money from them."

Zela drew in her breath.

And she felt that her voice sounded strange even to herself as she asked,

"How much?"

The Earl hesitated before with an effort he replied,

"Fifty thousand pounds!"

Zela could not prevent herself from giving a little cry of horror.

Then she said quickly,

"What has happened to all that money? How could you have lost it?"

"I lost it," the Earl replied, "because the Ruler of the country, who the Comtesse's friend was collaborating with, died unexpectedly."

"Died!" Zela exclaimed.

"It might have been a dagger's thrust or a natural affliction of his heart. Whatever it was only one thing is certain, the Ruler is dead and so are the transactions that have been passing between him and the Comtesse's friend in Paris."

"So you are saying, Papa," Zela said slowly, "that we have lost fifty thousand pounds."

"I can hardly believe it myself, but that is the exact amount of money that we now owe the bank and somehow, although God knows how, we will have to pay it back."

Zela felt as if the roof was collapsing in on her.

Then she wanted to scream.

She told herself that it would not help anyone and she had to be calm.

Above all she knew that she must not reproach her father for what he had done and so she kissed his cheek.

"It's very bad luck, Papa," she just managed to say. "But I am sure because you are so clever that you can do something if only to retrieve a little of the money that you invested. Do you know this man in France?"

"It's funny you should ask that question," the Earl said, "because I have been telling myself all the time I have been coming home that I should have gone out to Paris to see him, rather than just hand the money to the Comtesse and believe I would strike gold as she had done."

"Do you know who this man is?" Zela asked.

"I know his name and his address. It was only as I came up the drive just now, I decided that I would go to Paris at once, talk to him, man to man, to see if anything can be salvaged from the wreck."

"I think it a very sensible idea," Zela murmured.

Her father looked at her.

"Do you really mean that?"

"I think that it's something you should have done at once," Zela said. "Even before you came home. But even if he had been doing this business for some time and on a big scale, I cannot believe that it is not possible to get some of your money back from him."

She drew in her breath and went on more firmly,

"After all, if he was sending out your money to this Ruler, he might have been sending the same amount from a dozen other people."

She saw that he was listening and she carried on,

"The Ruler may have died, but, if a great deal of oil and anything else has already been despatched, it would be only fair and right for you to have a share of what that last consignment brought in."

"You are indeed a very clever girl," the Earl said. "It's exactly what I think myself. I was so stunned after what had happened I could only think that I must come home and wonder what we together can do about it."

"I think, Papa, it's not a question of wondering," Zela said, "but of taking action. If you don't make a claim, then this man in Paris, if he is honest, may easily divide any money he has received among all the other investors."

"Of course! Of course!" the Earl agreed. "I should have thought of that. But, because it was so horrifying and I knew that I had made a fool of myself, the only thing I could think of doing was to come back home."

"That was sensible. But now we have talked about it, Papa, the sooner you leave for Paris the better."

"I will go there tomorrow," the Earl said. "It will be quicker to go straight from here to Dover than to go back to London."

The way he spoke made Zela think that he did not wish to tell the Comtesse that he was going to Paris.

Aloud she asked him,

"Who else has invested money with this man?"

"I really have no idea," he replied. "Of course the Comtesse, being such a social success, knows very many people. But I thought that she was being particularly kind to me when she suggested that, if I could find the money, it would ensure that I would be a rich man very quickly."

"So you have no idea, Papa, that anyone else you know has received the bad news of what has occurred with the Ruler's death."

The Earl made an empty gesture with his hands.

"Because it was so secretive and not exactly above board, I did not think to ask the Comtesse if anyone else was involved. Actually, I think if they were, she would not have given me their names any more than she would give mine to them."

"I understand that, Papa," Zela muttered.

Then the Earl said rather pathetically,

"Just how can I ask you to forgive me, my dearest, when I have been so incredibly stupid? I know that you will suffer perhaps even more than I shall."

He gave a deep sigh.

"We have no money to pay the servants nor will we be able to keep the horses."

He was almost talking to himself, but Zela knew that every word he said was like a dagger in his chest as it was in hers.

How could they possibly go on living at The Hall without anyone to cook or serve them?

How could the country be anything but unbearable without the horses?

Then she told herself that it was no use looking so far ahead. What she had to do was to get her father to Paris as soon as possible and then he must find out if there is any money left and if he could claim his share of it.

She kissed the Earl on the cheek again and rose to her feet.

"I am going upstairs," she said, "to pack the clothes you will want in Paris. I expect that most of them are in the trunk you brought down from London or did you leave them behind?"

"I brought back everything I possess," the Earl said slowly. "I have told the porter that I no longer require my flat."

Zela could not think of anything to say and then she remarked,

"I expect Brunt will have taken your cases upstairs by now. I don't expect you will be away, Papa, for more than a week, but in case things take a little longer I will pack enough shirts to last you for a fortnight."

She was standing in front of him and he then bent forward to take her hand in both of his.

"Forgive my, my dearest. I know that I have made a fool of myself. You know how ashamed I am and it's so kind of you not to reproach me."

"Why should I?" Zela asked. "I am trying to make things easier for us and perhaps it will not be quite as bad as it seems at present."

She hesitated for a moment and then she said,

"What I don't understand is whether you wrote out a cheque for the money or gave it to the Comtesse and if so, who was it made payable to?"

"That is something that I should have explained to you," the Earl replied. "Because everything was kept as secretive as possible, the money was handed over in cash."

"In cash!" Zela exclaimed in surprise.

"Large notes! It was, the Comtesse said, the only possible way for me to participate in the operation and remain anonymous. I thought at the time that it was very sensible of her."

"Was there anything to prove that the money which was sent to Paris was yours?" Zela asked.

"Oh, I expect the Comtesse told Monsieur Henri Monte, which is the man's name, who I am," he replied. "But it was important that no one else should know who was taking part in case the officials in the Ruler's country objected to what he was doing."

"I am sure they would have done," Zela said a little bitterly. "At least you know Monsieur Henri's name and where he lives. So, Papa, you must go to him as quickly as you possibly can."

"I am aware of that now," he remarked. "It was very foolish of me to come home. Quite frankly, when the Comtesse told me last night what had happened, actually it was in the early hours of the morning, the only thing I wanted to do was to get away from London as quickly as I possibly could."

Zela felt that he was just like a child running back to his mother because he was hurt.

Once again she kissed him.

"You are not to blame yourself, Papa," she insisted. "What we have to think of now is how much we can save.

Perhaps when you arrive in Paris things will not be as bad as they seem."

Her voice became bitter as she added,

"It would be just like the French to make the British bear the brunt of a catastrophe to get their countrymen off as lightly as possible."

As she finished speaking, she remembered that the Comtesse, who was at the bottom of all this trouble, was French and her father might resent anything that was said against her.

He was sitting forward on the sofa forlornly with his head in his hands.

"Drink your brandy, Papa," Zela urged, giving it to him. "When you have done so, you must tell Armstrong in the stables that you want him to drive you to the Station first thing tomorrow morning."

She smiled at him as she continued,

"I am sure that there will be a train leaving early to take you to Dover. With a bit of luck you will be in Paris tomorrow night."

As she finished speaking, Zela opened the door of the study.

She looked back at the Earl, but said nothing. She went out of the room and started to run down the passage to the hall.

And she knew that at the moment her father was in the same state as he had been after her mother's death.

He was finding it very difficult to think of anything sensibly and he was suffering within himself.

She must make him take decisive action.

Then she knew that he would do everything in his power to make the Frenchman give him back some of the money and that would be obviously better than nothing.

'We have to do this quickly,' she thought as she ran up the stairs.

She walked towards her father's bedroom.

As she did so the full horror of what had occurred seemed to sweep over her like a dark cloud.

How could it be possible?

How could she ever have anticipated that her father would do anything so utterly disastrous and damaging?

He had mortgaged everything they possessed and had lost a sum of money that seemed to her too enormous to even contemplate.

The situation they were in was so horrifying that there was only one hope and it was that in some miraculous way God would save them.

As Zela entered her father's bedroom, the first thing she saw was a picture of her mother. It had been painted soon after they were married and hung over the fireplace.

Zela stood still in front of it and thought, as she had thought many times, how beautiful her mother had been.

'Mama would understand what a desperate position we are in at this moment,' she told herself silently.

She put her hands together and began to pray.

As she prayed she realised that unless God helped them they were lost.

'Please God help us please, *please*!' she whispered beneath her breath.

She felt as she spoke that her mother was saying the same thing.

CHAPTER TWO

Zela was downstairs half an hour before her father the next morning.

She made certain that he was offered all the dishes for breakfast that he really enjoyed.

Armstrong was waiting in the post chaise with two of their fastest horses to take him to the Railway Station.

He had been very gloomy at dinner and Zela had great difficulty trying to coax him to talk about anything and the disaster had clearly overwhelmed him.

Finally, when Zela had gone up to her bedroom, she felt completely exhausted.

She knew, however, that she had won the battle to insist that her father should go at once to Paris and she felt quite certain that once he was actually there he would find someone who would help him.

He knew Paris well and he had been there often as a young man and she thought if nothing else the bubbling *joie de vivre*, which everyone felt in Paris, would cheer him up.

It was a silent and depressing drive to the Station.

Zela had looked up the time of a train to Canterbury and from there the Earl could change into one of the trains that went to Dover almost every hour.

"I am quite sure, Papa," she said again, as she had yesterday, "that you will be safely in Paris tonight."

The Earl did not answer her and she knew that he was thinking that there would be nobody to help him when he did arrive there.

"I will stay at the Travellers Club," he commented, "unless I can find somewhere cheaper."

The train came into the Station and Zela kissed him goodbye affectionately and urged him,

"Don't worry, dearest Papa, take very good care of yourself. I have a feeling that things will not be as bad as we think and that our prayers will be answered."

"I only hope you are right," her father replied in a deep voice.

He kissed her again and climbed into the train.

As they had to economise, he was travelling Second Class instead of First.

He waved rather limply to Zela as the train moved off and out of sight.

Then she turned and went back to where Armstrong was waiting for her.

She realised, just like the other servants, that he was curious as to why the Earl, coming home after being away for quite some time, had left again so hurriedly.

She had merely said to Brunt that her father had an important engagement in Paris.

'That is not a lie,' she told herself, 'it's very very important to us.'

They drove off and Armstrong then asked,

"Be there a chance, my Lady, of you speakin' to 'is Lordship about the 'orses?"

"No, it was impossible to do that last night," Zela replied. "My father was tired and had so many other issues on his mind."

"Well, you mustn't forget then when 'is Lordship comes back 'ome," Armstrong persisted.

Zela gave a deep sigh.

Unless he had good news it would not be a question of having new horses. They would not be able to afford to keep the ones they already had in the stable.

She did not say anything aloud, but to change the subject, she asked,

"When you were last in London with Papa, were the carriages very impressive? I think that there are some new designs around that His Royal Highness the Prince of Wales is using."

"They be that smart," Armstrong replied, "that you wonder if they be part of a play or even a circus!"

Zela laughed.

"They sound very flamboyant."

"They be all right and a little bit more, my Lady. One of the smartest belongs to that foreign lady who be friends with 'is Lordship."

"You mean the Comtesse de Courché," Zela said. "I am told she is very pretty."

"So they all be sayin'," Armstrong replied at once. "Her coachman were a-tellin' me that people stood on the seats in Hyde Park to see 'er pass."

He chuckled and went on,

"If 'e stops the carriage, there be a crowd round it afore 'e can say 'Jack Robinson'."

"She must be very beautiful," Zela said.

She was thinking that she hated the Comtesse.

She was the one who had been instrumental, even if she had not meant to be, in allowing her father to lose so much money.

"I 'ears too when I be in London," Armstrong went on, "that the lady, maybe 'cos 'er be French, 'as difficulty in keepin' staff at 'er 'ouse."

"I can understand that," Zela said. "The English always find it problematic working for foreigners."

"That be true," he agreed. "And it's sommat I'd not care for, I can tell you that, my Lady."

Zela did not like to think that perhaps in a very short space of time Armstrong himself would be looking for another place to work.

He had been with them for over twenty years and was excellent with the horses and never complained when they were short-handed.

As she could not bear to think about losing him, she said quickly,

"What else did you hear about the Comtesse?"

"I 'ears, my Lady, that 'er cook 'ad walked out in an 'uff and 'er were now a-lookin' for a secretary."

"A secretary!" Zela exclaimed in surprise.

She had thought that it was only men who required secretaries to help them with their correspondence and the one her father employed acted as manager of the estate as well.

He paid all the staff wages on Fridays and had been at Langdale Hall since her grandfather's time. And he was getting old although he was still very efficient.

She was wondering now with a growing feeling of horror that perhaps Mr. Johnson would have to leave, as well as the other members of their staff.

'Oh, please, God, don't let that happen to us,' she prayed. 'How can we possibly manage without the people who always look after us?'

"Now you've brought it to me memory," continued Armstrong, "this 'ere coachman then asked me if there be anyone around 'ere who'd make a good secretary for 'is Mistress. She says she didn't like Londoners, they be too curious and 'er didn't trust 'em."

Zela thought this was a rather strange thing to say.

Then suddenly it struck her and it was almost as if someone was telling her exactly what to do.

If she applied for the position of secretary to the Comtesse, she might be able to find out how and why her father had invested all this money in the first place.

He had gone to Paris to see if there was anything left of the wreck and she might well find exactly the same in London.

Aloud she said,

"So when did you hear this from the Comtesse's coachman, Armstrong?"

"Now let me see, my Lady, must 'ave been the last time I takes 'is Lordship up to London."

He went on as if he was looking back in his mind,

"Instead of goin' straight to them rooms 'e was in, 'is Lordship goes to Berkeley Square where that Frenchie lady 'as an 'ouse."

Zela knew that they were not very far apart and she then asked,

"Do you know why my father went there first?"

"I thinks, my Lady, it were 'cos 'e knows that the French lady be a-goin' out. If 'e calls later, 'er wouldn't be at 'ome."

Zela smiled.

"So her carriage was waiting outside and that was when you talked to her coachman, Armstrong?"

"Aye, that be it," he agreed. "I was admirin' the 'orses. Them must've cost a pile of money and any man'd be pleased to drive 'em."

"It was then the coachman said that the Comtesse was looking for a secretary?" Zela asked.

She wanted to be quite certain that what Armstrong had told her was the truth.

"Aye, that be it, as I tells you, my Lady, 'e wonders if there'd be anyone from these parts who'd like to go to London."

"I expect there are plenty if we only knew of them," Zela said.

She drew in her breath because she was thinking quickly.

Then she said,

"I am sure that his Lordship will want to help his friend, the Comtesse. I think the best thing I can do would be to speak to her myself and find out exactly what she requires."

She paused as if she was thinking and then went on,

"I know someone in the next village who is looking for a job, but then I must be quite sure of what is required before I recommend anyone."

"If you asks me," Armstrong said, "I thinks that Frenchie lady'd be real difficult to please. I've been to that there 'ouse many times and there always be different servants there to when I've been afore and there be plenty of complainin', I can tell you that!"

"That is why I must be very careful about who I do recommend," Zela added. "If I catch the midday train to London, I will be there by one-thirty and I can come back on the five o'clock."

Armstrong thought this over carefully.

"Aye," he said finally, "your Ladyship can do that if that's what you wants to do."

"I think that it might be helpful and I expect the Comtesse has asked his Lordship to recommend someone local, but, of course, having to go to Paris so quickly he forgot to tell me about it."

Armstrong had nothing more to add and they drove on in silence.

It was only when they had reached Langdale Hall that Armstrong asked,

"So you be goin' up to London today, my Lady?"

"Yes, I am. Please bring the horses round at about a quarter past eleven. If I miss that train there will not be another one until late this afternoon."

"That be true," Armstrong agreed. "I'll be on time, my Lady. You can count on it."

Once Zela was back in the house she went upstairs to her bedroom.

She was thinking that what she was doing was very unusual and such a course of action would never even have entered her head in the past.

Yet, because they were in such a desperate position, she felt that she had to do something positive.

Perhaps, although she might very well be mistaken, being with the Comtesse would give her a clue as to what had really happened to her father's money.

Zela could not help thinking that it was all so very strange. In fact it was most peculiar that, at the moment her father had actually handed over such a very large sum, the Ruler in the East had died.

As the money had obviously not reached him, then someone else must be holding on to it now.

The more Zela thought it over, the more it seemed to her extremely mysterious.

Unless the person the money had been given to by the Comtesse was a complete crook and a rogue, he would have naturally returned her father's fifty thousand pounds by now.

Alternatively he would at least have offered her Papa the goods that he had bought with it.

'I don't understand business,' Zela said to herself. 'At the same time there is obviously something going on to which no one has given a proper explanation.'

She knew that she was acting on an impulse and yet her brain told her that the Comtesse must know more than she had told her father.

'It might be a wasted journey,' Zela thought as she started to change her clothes, 'but then at least I am doing something rather than moping around miserably and being despondent.'

The truth was that she did not really want to think about what they must do if the money was really lost.

The contents of Langdale Hall and the horses were all entailed onto the next Earl and, as her father had no son, this was a distant cousin they very seldom saw.

It was no use thinking therefore that they could sell off the family paintings, which were extremely valuable, as was the antique furniture.

There would indeed be a little money if they sold her mother's jewels, which had been left to her, but Zela knew that she would hate to part with them.

She was still not quite certain what she was doing, yet her instinct, which was very strong and which she had used all her life, told her that she had to take some positive action.

Crying over spilt milk helped no one.

So, with a determined look on her face, she went to the wardrobe to take down her best dress and coat to travel to London in.

She could not possibly go to the Comtesse as her father's daughter.

And she had to be a complete stranger to be given the position of a secretary.

Of course, as she was arriving after luncheon, the Comtesse might not be at home, in which case she would have had the journey for nothing.

Now that she was thinking more clearly Zela knew that, if she was to apply for the position, she had to work out every detail.

She would find out nothing unless she was living in the house and was accepted as one of the staff.

So instead of taking out her best dress from the wardrobe, Zela started first to pack her case.

She put in clothes that she thought would be most suitable for a secretary. They must be modest, plain and simple as befitted someone who worked for her living.

That, Zela thought with a little smile, was easier for her to find than if she had wanted to be smart or up to date and it would have been impossible for her, as her mother's daughter, not to have very good taste.

Going to the small writing desk in her bedroom, she quickly wrote two references for herself.

She had first to think of a suitable name for herself.

She knew at once that it would be easier for her to remember if she called herself 'Lane' instead of 'Lang'.

Her second name that she had been christened with was 'Mary' and so 'Mary Lane' was exactly right for the young woman she was going to pretend to be.

'I will say that my father is a Vicar,' she thought with a smile. 'That at least is respectable!'

She then wrote herself a glowing reference from Lady Fairhaven's comptroller.

Her Ladyship had died, which was why Mary Lane was no longer in her employment.

The same applied to the second reference she wrote out, which was from the Adjutant of General Sir Arthur Woodward.

Miss Lane had been obliged to give up her post with him because he was in ill health. The doctors had said that his sons must do everything that was required and he must not be consulted on anything that might trouble him.

It was unfortunate, Zela thought, that the writing paper was not headed. As that was impossible, she merely wrote in the names of the grand houses of those who had recommended her.

She was sure that a foreigner would not bother to check to see if the people she had mentioned were real, while an Englishman or woman might easily look them up in *Debrett's Peerage.*

Zela put the references in her handbag and then, adding her brush and comb to the things that were already in her case, she closed it.

She then went to find Brunt to carry it downstairs for her.

"You're going away, my Lady?" he asked her with a surprised air.

"At the last moment his Lordship asked me to do one or two things for him in London that he had forgotten about," Zela replied to him. "As soon as they are complete I will come home, but it may take a day or two, so don't worry if I am not back by Saturday."

"You're going to London on your own, my Lady?" Brunt asked. "Surely you should have someone with you?"

Zela guessed that Brunt would be rather shocked at that, as her father had never allowed her to travel anywhere without being accompanied by a maid.

The only maid resident in the house at the moment was Maria, who had been there for years, and Zela knew that she would never make herself ready for London so quickly as she suffered from arthritis.

"I shall be quite all right," she said to Brunt. "I am being met at Victoria Station by friends."

Brunt shook his head.

"It's just not right, my Lady," he said, "for you to be travelling alone. But then things be changing and not for the better I thinks."

"You are not to worry about me," Zela urged him. "I will send you a letter telling you exactly when I want to return so that you can arrange for Armstrong to meet me at the Station."

"Well, all I can say, my Lady, is that you must take care of yourself," Brunt said. "There be things going on in London that we wouldn't tolerate here in our village. I'm surprised that his Lordship should let you go away without him."

"I will be back long before his Lordship returns, so what he does not know will not worry him," Zela replied.

Brunt then brought her case down the stairs and, as he placed it in the chaise, he was still shaking his head with disapproval.

"I know you will look after everything until I get back," Zela said, "and I promise you that I will be as quick as I possibly can."

"You take good care of yourself, my Lady," Brunt said again looking worried.

She knew as she turned away that he did not know what on earth the world was coming to! Ladies of Quality had never gone anywhere without a chaperone.

Armstrong drove Zela to Canterbury Station.

The Stationmaster, who, of course, she knew well, was also surprised that she was travelling alone.

"I'll put you in a carriage for 'Ladies Only'," he said, "and, if there be no one else there, I'll lock you in, my Lady."

"That is very kind of you," Zela replied. "I know that my father, if he was with me, would be most grateful."

"I only hopes his Lordship has no trouble in gettin' to Paris," the Stationmaster said. "I wouldn't trust them Frenchie trains. Foreigners can't arrange things as we do."

Zela agreed with him.

However, as the train came puffing into the Station and she climbed into it, she was thinking that it was the French who had taken their money from them.

And it was going to be very difficult to persuade them to give it back.

All the way to London she was planning in detail in her mind what she would say to the Comtesse.

*

The Hackney carriage duly set her down outside the Comtesse's house in Berkeley Square.

By this time she was not only nervous but rather intimidated.

How could she have ever imagined two days ago that she would now find herself seeking employment as a secretary in London?

She had been looking forward to her father's return and being very happy riding the horses.

She then asked the driver of the Hackney carriage to wait with her luggage.

"Be you a-goin' to be long, miss?" he enquired.

"I hope not," Zela replied. "But I may have to go straight back to Victoria Station."

"I'll wait," he said grudgingly, "but then you'll 'ave to pay me extra time for me a-doin' so."

Zela nodded and she thought that he looked a little more cheerful. He then said in a different tone of voice,

"Don't you worry, miss. It be cool 'ere as there be shade for the old 'orse."

Zela smiled at him and then rang the bell.

The door was opened at once by a footman in what she thought was a very ostentatious livery.

A butler came from behind him and looked at Zela rather quizzically.

"Is it at all possible for me to see the Comtesse de Courché?" she enquired. "I understand that she requires a secretary and I am applying for the position."

The butler seemed surprised and then he said in a different tone of voice to the one he would have used if she had been herself.

"In that case you'd better come in. Madame is just about to go out, but perhaps she'll see you."

He said 'Madame' in an affected accent to make it sound French.

"Oh, do be very kind and persuade her to do so," Zela said pleadingly. "I have come all the way up from the country because I was told that this position was vacant."

As she looked so pretty, the butler's eyes softened a little.

He pointed to a chair at the side of the mantelpiece in the hall and suggested,

"Sit you down, miss, and I'll see what I can do."

"Thank you. Thank you very much," Zela said.

He walked away.

The footman, realising immediately that she was of no importance, scratched his head after the butler had shut the door.

"I don't suppose you'll stay long," he said in a low voice.

Zela managed to look intrigued.

"Why not?" she asked.

"'Er be a foreigner," the footman said, jerking his thumb towards the end of the hall. "'Er wants this and 'er wants that and we be on the run all day from mornin' till night."

"It does sound rather frightening," Zela said softly. "But I hope to be sitting at a desk."

The footman gave what sounded rather like a bitter laugh.

"You'll be lucky. It be 'fetch this thing and fetch that', until you don't know if you be on your 'ead or your 'eels."

Zela laughed.

As she did so, the butler returned.

"Madame la Comtesse will see you," he said, "but you'll have to be quick about it as she's goin' out shortly."

Zela rose to her feet.

She followed the butler as he walked a short way down a passage and then stopped to open a door into what was obviously the library. It was an attractive room with many books on the walls and an elegant writing table by the window.

Just rising from it was an elaborately dressed, very beautiful woman.

She was not very tall, but her body was perfectly proportioned.

Her dark hair elegantly arranged on top of her head gave her a dignity which she might otherwise not have had.

Her eyes were dark and large and her skin had not the clearness or whiteness of an Englishwoman.

In point of fact her features were perfect, but she was indisputably French.

Zela crossed the room.

And, as she did so, the Comtesse looked her up and down in what was a slightly insulting manner.

"Why have you come to see me?" she asked almost sharply.

"I have heard, *madame*, from a friend who lives in London," Zela replied, "that you require a secretary. As I have unfortunately been required to leave the place where I was working because Lord Fairhaven was too ill to need me, I came to London to see if I could help you in any way."

"You can help me," the Comtesse said, "if you are good at your job. The last secretary had no idea how to address His Royal Highness the Prince of Wales."

As she was speaking, the Comtesse sat down in a chair, but she left Zela standing.

"As I have been, as I have just told you, *madame*," Zela went on, "with Lord Fairhaven and also General Sir Arthur Woodward I am fully accustomed to writing letters to Royalty as well as to English aristocrats."

"Let me see their recommendations," the Comtesse demanded harshly.

Zela took her references out of her handbag and handed them over.

The Comtesse looked at them carefully and with an expression that told Zela she wanted to find fault.

It passed through her mind that it was a good thing that she had been clever enough to alter her handwriting.

If the two letters had been written in the same hand, she was quite certain that the Comtesse would have noticed it, although it might not have occurred to anyone else.

"These seem satisfactory," the Comtesse said when she had read them. "You are free now?"

"I have come up from the country, *madame*," Zela told her, "but I have brought enough clothes to last me for a week should you want me to start work right away."

She thought, although she did not say so, that the Comtesse looked relieved.

"If that is so," she said, "I will engage you. But if you are not as capable as you say you are, then you will leave without being paid for any work that you have done in the meantime. Is that clear?"

"Perfectly clear, *madame*," Zela responded.

"Very well," the Comtesse said, "you are engaged. The first thing you can do is to look through that pile of letters on my desk."

She paused a moment and then went on,

"Accept those where I have written an 'A' on the envelope and refuse those I have marked with an 'R'. Do you understand?"

"Absolutely, *madame*, and thank you very much for saying that you will engage me."

"I expect you to work hard," the Comtesse said, "as there is a great deal to do. And, of course. everything that happens here is strictly private. You don't talk to anyone, not even to a close relative, about me, my possessions or anyone who visits me."

She did not wait for Zela to answer but went on,

"If I ever find that you are disobeying me, you will leave here immediately without any reference and without any pay."

"I understand, *madame*," Zela said. "And I assure you that the two distinguished people I have worked for trusted me completely."

"Let's hope that I can do the same," the Comtesse replied.

She rose to her feet and rang a gold bell that stood on the writing table.

The butler opened the door almost immediately and Zela felt that he must have been listening outside.

"You rang, *madame*?" he asked.

"This young woman is engaged as my secretary," the Comtesse said. "Her name – "

She looked down at the two references that she was still holding in her hand.

" – is Mary Lane. And she will be known in the household as 'Miss Lane' and she will take her meals in the housekeeper's room."

The butler gave a little bow.

"Very good, *madame*."

"Now I have to leave," the Comtesse said. "I am already late for my next engagement. Don't forget who is coming to dinner tonight and make sure that we have the vintage champagne and the best brandy."

"It's all been seen to, *madame*," the butler intoned.

Without a single word to Zela the Comtesse then swept out of the room.

She left behind her an exotic and what Zela knew to be a very expensive perfume.

The butler did not close the door behind her.

Zela walked towards the writing table.

She thought with a little thrill of excitement that she had succeeded.

She had found a way into the Comtesse's house and she could not prevent an image of the Trojan Horse and the Ancients Greeks from coming into her mind.

Now she had to find, which for the moment seemed impossible, something however small that would help her father.

She did not sit down at the writing table, as she knew that the butler, having seen the Comtesse drive away, would expect her to pay the cabbie and collect her luggage from the Hackney carriage.

He came back a few minutes later.

"Well, you're in, Miss Lane," he said, "and don't blame me if you find it not to your likin'."

"I am very delighted, for the moment, to have a position," Zela replied. "It's not easy in the country to find someone who wants a secretary. Most people will have a manager for their estate who also does any secretarial work that may be required in the house."

"I know that," the butler said. "I was with the Earl of Yarmouth for many years. Ever such a nice gentleman he be. Never a cross word and there weren't a person on his estate who didn't want to make him happy."

"That is what we all want," Zela remarked.

"It don't cost anythin' to hope," the butler replied. "Come along, miss, and pay off your cabbie. It costs more every minute he's standin' out there."

Zela laughed and followed him into the hall.

She paid the cabbie, giving him a tip that made him touch his hat.

"Thanks, miss," he said. "It be a real pleasure to drive someone so pretty."

"That's the only nice compliment I have had since I came to London," Zela sighed.

"Then you'll get a lot more," the cabbie rambled on. "Just you wait and see."

"I do hope so, but I am not too optimistic!" Zela replied.

One of the footmen on the butler's instructions had by now taken her case out of the Hackney carriage and was carrying it into the house.

The driver whipped up his horse and, as he turned away and Zela waved to him, he swept off his hat.

She thought to herself that if everybody was as nice as him the world would be a much better place.

When she went into the house, the footman led the way up the stairs.

As they reached the first floor an elderly woman was waiting. She was not dressed as a housekeeper, but was wearing a frilled cap and apron.

Before she could speak the footman said,

"This be the new secretary."

Zela held out her hand.

"My name is Mary Lane," she said, "and Madame la Comtesse has engaged me to take care of her letters."

"You've taken on a big job," the woman said. "I just 'opes you'll settle down with us 'ere, so to speak. I'm Hannah."

She took Zela's hand rather limply as she spoke.

"And I hope so too," Zela replied. "I would be very grateful if you would show me where I am to sleep."

"There be a little room at the end 'ere which no one ever uses," Hannah answered. "I thinks that you'll be more comfortable there."

"That is very kind of you, Hannah. As I will have to come up and down the stairs quite a lot, it will be more convenient if I am on this floor."

Hannah walked ahead and, as she had said, at the end of the corridor there was a small room.

Zela thought that it was really a dressing room and was meant for a man. It contained a bed, a wardrobe and a washstand.

The dressing table, which was in the window, was merely a table with a cloth over it.

41

"You'll be quiet 'ere," Hannah said, "and Madame, as we're told to call 'er, don't like anyone walkin' about at night. So stay where you be and don't go pokin' about the stairs."

"I will certainly take your advice," Zela smiled.

She thanked the footman for bringing her case up and, when she had unlocked it, she then turned and said to Hannah,

"I think before I start any unpacking I should go down and see to Madame's letters. There is a huge pile for me to answer and it's going to take time."

"She'll expect them done," Hannah said, "afore she returns from wherever she's gone."

The way she spoke told Zela that Hannah disliked her Mistress.

She thought that it was rather strange that anyone so beautiful should manage to create so much dissension in her household.

However she said nothing.

Hannah watched her take off her hat and the short coat that matched the black dress underneath it.

"I'd expect," she said as Zela looked in the mirror, "you'd like to see the 'ouse while you've got the chance and know which room be which."

"That would be very helpful," Zela replied.

"Then come along," Hannah said. "I belongs to the 'ouse, so to speak."

"What do you mean by that?" Zela asked her.

"Well then, I were 'ere with the last two owners," Hannah replied, "and when the 'ouse were empty I stayed on till it were rented again by the Comtesse. 'Cos I knows me way about 'ere she was glad to 'ave me."

"I am sure she was," Zela said. "Especially as she is French."

Hannah gave a brief chuckle.

"That's a difficulty, I can tell you. The girls I 'as under me don't like being snapped at by a Frenchie. They would take it from one of us, but not from a foreigner."

"It must make it very difficult for you," Zela said.

"Difficult!" Hannah exclaimed. "As soon as I've got someone to do what I wants, along comes Madame and upsets 'er. There be plenty of jobs empty in London now and, if them young'un's don't like the one they be in, out they goes! Then the likes of me 'as to start all over again at the beginnin'."

"That must be a bother," Zela said sympathetically.

"Now if you wants to stay," Hannah went on, "you just 'as to agree with whatever Madame says. If you argue, she shouts at you and you'll find yourself outside the front door afore you can say 'knife'."

Zela thought that this was all very peculiar.

It certainly did not match with the flattering articles that had been written about the Comtesse in the women's magazines.

Zela supposed that however difficult the Comtesse was with her staff, she was very different when she was with someone like her father.

"Now this 'ere be Madame's bedroom," Hannah was saying, opening a door. "You can see it's what you might call a 'Temple of Love'."

There was a distinct sharpness in her voice.

And it told Zela that she disapproved strongly of the Comtesse and even more of her love affairs.

The room was certainly very glamorous.

It had a carved golden four-poster bed draped with muslin curtains and the exquisite furniture must have come from Italy.

The paintings on the wall were mostly French in very elegant frames and the large mirror on the dressing table was a riot of carved gold cupids. They were climbing up to what Zela thought must be 'The Goddess of Love'.

There were expensive orchids on the tables and in the fireplace and a negligee thrown over one of the chairs was a mass of frills and bows of satin ribbon.

Because she realised that Hannah was waiting for her to approve, Zela commented,

"It's very glamorous."

"That's just 'ow we 'as to keep it," Hannah added. "One thing out of place and there's a row that shakes the very roof!"

Zela thought that it was best not to say anything more.

She was next shown the Comtesse's boudoir, which was as elaborate as her bedroom.

Then Hannah escorted her downstairs.

"I never asked you," she said, "if, as you'd come up from the country, you'd 'ad anythin' to eat."

"I was in much too much of a hurry to think of eating," Zela admitted.

"I'll go and get you somethin' and a cup of tea right away," Hannah volunteered. "Go into the 'ousekeeper's room. I expect you've guessed the 'ousekeeper be what I'm supposed to be, though I don't get paid as one!"

"I am very sure that you would make a wonderful housekeeper," Zela said. "And I would like to see you in rustling black with a silver chatelaine at your waist!"

Hannah giggled.

"That'll be the day. An 'ousemaid be cheaper than an 'ousekeeper and that's all them as engages us thinks about."

Hannah took Zela into the housekeeper's room. It was small, but quite adequately furnished.

She then went down the backstairs to the kitchen and surprisingly quickly Zela was brought a plate of cold ham, a cheese sandwich and a mug of tea.

Because Zela was so relieved at securing the job she wanted, she was quite hungry.

She was feeling very different to the way that she had felt when she had had breakfast.

As she was eating, Hannah continued to chat away endlessly.

As Zela expected, she soon spoke of the gentlemen the Comtesse entertained.

"They comes one after another," she was saying. "It be 'er beauty as draws 'em and I often thinks to meself they wouldn't be so eager if they knows what she be like when they weren't about."

"I have seen her name mentioned very often in *The Court Circular*," Zela murmured.

"'She enjoys that and cuts out and keeps everythin' they says about 'er in the newspapers," Hannah answered. "She likes to 'ave men with titles fussin' all over 'er. But then most women in London be like that."

"I am sure, because the Comtesse is so beautiful, that there are plenty of men to tell her so."

Hannah laughed.

"You bet there be. The last one was the Earl of Langdale and 'e were never out of the 'ouse. Ever so nice 'e be and kind too, which be unlike some of 'em."

"Where is the Earl now?" Zela asked.

45

She hoped that it sounded a casual question which anyone might ask.

There was silence for a moment.

Then Hannah glanced over her shoulder as if she was afraid that someone might be listening to her.

"Somethin' queer 'appened to 'im," she said. "Just as it's 'appened to them others. They be payin' 'er flashy compliments, laughin' and with 'er day and night and then sudden like afore any of us knows it, they be gone and we never sees 'em again."

"What *did* happen?" Zela asked.

Hannah shook her head.

"I don't know and that's the truth. It all 'appens so quick and then 'e's gone without even a single goodbye."

"I cannot – understand it," Zela said nervously.

"Nor can I," Hannah muttered. "'Twas the Earl as went that way and three others afore 'im."

Zela did not like to ask her any more questions or appear to be too interested.

At the same time it merely added to her conviction that something was very wrong.

She had at that moment no idea what it could be and yet from what Hannah had told her what had happened to her father had happened to other men.

Could they have lost their money too?

It did not seem possible.

Yet why, if Hannah was telling her the truth, did they suddenly disappear out of the Comtesse's life?

She put down the mug of tea she was holding in her hand.

"I think," she said, "if I want to stay here and not get into trouble on my first day, I should do some work."

"Yes, you should get on," Hannah replied, "and try to keep Madame 'appy. It be a long time since I've 'ad anyone like you to talk to and I only 'opes you'll stay on 'ere with us."

"I hope so as well, Hannah, but, of course, I can see that everything depends on Madame."

CHAPTER THREE

The Marquis of Buckwood walked into White's Club.

He had been away for three years and was pleased when the porter welcomed him,

"Good morning, my Lord. It's so nice to see you back."

"Thank you, James," the Marquis replied. "Are any of my particular friends in the Club this morning?"

The porter hesitated for a moment and then he said,

"Mr. Windell is in the Coffee Room."

"Good!" the Marquis exclaimed.

He thought that it was just like home coming back to White's.

When he had last been here, he had not inherited his title, yet the porter had not only remembered him but knew that he was now higher up on the Social Ladder.

He walked into the Coffee Room where there was a sprinkling of men he did not know.

Then at the far end of the room he saw his friend, Charles Windell.

They had been good friends at Eton and Oxford University and had joined the same Regiment.

When they were on leave, they spent much of their time enjoying themselves in London.

Then the Marquis had gone to India at the special request of the Viceroy, who was a friend of his father's.

He was in those days just Rupert Wood, as he had an elder brother, who had been killed in a hunting accident, but there had been no point in the Marquis returning home.

He was, in point of fact, heavily engaged in *The Great Game,* the deadliest Secret Service in the world.

The English had invented it to stop and turn back the Russians, who were attempting to conquer most of Asia and were then planning to encircle India.

It was extremely dangerous, but at the same time it was exciting and the Marquis had enjoyed it to the full.

There had been moments when he thought that his end had come and there was no chance of his surviving. Yet by a miracle he had saved himself and the lives of a great number of British soldiers.

"If I could give you a medal," the Viceroy had said to him, "you know I would do so. But, as no one must ever know how brilliant you have been, all I can say is 'thank you' for myself, Queen Victoria and the people of India."

The Marquis had smiled.

"That is all I want," he had murmured.

After this episode he was told to keep quiet and to spend as much time as possible in Viceregal House.

Then his father died. It was not surprising as he had been in poor health for some time. In fact he had never recovered from the death of his eldest son.

And it meant that Rupert Wood was now the fifth Marquis of Buckwood and his life in the Army and in *The Great Game* was at an abrupt end.

"We will miss you," the Viceroy had said to him. "At the same time we can never be certain that you are not a marked man. Quite frankly the sooner you leave India the safer you will be."

The Marquis had then come home, but he knew that he would miss not only his Regiment but the excitement of pitting his brain against the scheming Russians.

He had certainly played a major part in preventing them from conquering India by stealth rather than by force of arms.

The Marquis had now been at home for six months and he was trying to cope with the massive amount there was to do following his father's death.

Buckwood Park was a particularly large estate in the County of Suffolk with more estates in other Counties.

But because of his father's extended illness a great many things had been neglected and the Marquis was well aware that an enormous amount of new machinery, new plans and ideas were desperately needed.

They had to be introduced if the Buckwood estate was to be modernised and the Marquis was determined that it would be.

There was so much to be done on the farms and the estate cottages needed extensive repairing and restoration.

He had spent six months travelling from one estate to the other and he was just beginning to feel that things were now moving in the right direction.

Even so he would not have come to London if he had not received an invitation from the Prince of Wales.

It was to a dinner party that was like enumerable other parties that His Royal Highness had hosted.

Yet on the Marquis's invitation there had been a personal note saying that H.R.H. wished to see him and the Marquis thought that in the circumstances the only thing he could do would be to go to London.

He had arrived last night to stay in the vast house in Berkeley Square that his family had owned for many years.

The Marquis had been away for a long time and so he decided that what he should do was to find out what was happening from one of his friends.

Indeed nothing could be better than finding Charles Windell in White's at this very moment.

As the Marquis walked up to him, he realised that Charles was sitting in an armchair.

His fingers were touching his forehead and his eyes were closed.

For a moment the Marquis just stood still looking at him and then he asked,

"Are you asleep, Charles, or concentrating on some exquisite creature you met last night?"

Charles Windell opened his eyes.

When he saw who was speaking he gave a shout,

"Rupert! I had no idea you were in London."

"I only arrived last night," the Marquis said, sitting down beside him. "I thought this morning that I had better come to White's so as to hear all the latest gossip and, of course, who the beauty might be who is making you look so serious."

"As it happens it's very serious," Charles said in a gloomy voice. "But tell me first about yourself, Rupert, and I am so sorry that your father has passed away."

"He had been very ill for a long time," the Marquis replied. "So in a way it was a merciful release, but it has left me with an appalling amount to do."

"I quite understand," Charles said. "It's always the same when someone has been ill for a long time before they die."

"That is so true. But I have had an invitation from H.R.H. and felt that it would be rude to refuse."

"Of course it would," Charles agreed, "and he has always been fond of you."

"I am only astonished that he remembers me after my being away so long," the Marquis remarked. "I feel like a new boy at school. You must tell me who holds the cards these days and who is the talk of Rotten Row."

Charles gave a somewhat feeble laugh.

"You will learn all that soon enough," he replied. "By the way would you like a drink? But, if you want one, you will have to pay for it."

The Marquis raised his eyebrows.

"What has happened, Charles?"

"If you want the full horrible truth, at the moment I am completely and absolutely broke! I am trying to think what I can do about it."

The Marquis edged his chair nearer to his friend.

"Tell me about it," he suggested.

It was passing through his mind that Charles had never been rich, but his father owned a house and a small estate in Hertfordshire.

It was where the Windell family had lived for about a hundred years, but it did not in any way compare with the Buckwood possessions.

However he had stayed with Charles when they had been on leave from the Regiment and his father, who was a retired General, seemed comfortable and had several good horses that he could go hunting on.

As Charles did not answer at once, the Marquis said quietly,

"Tell me from the beginning what has gone wrong."

"My mother has been under the doctors for over a year," Charles began, "and it has proved most expensive. My father was hoping that he would be able to afford some new horses and we talked about it when I was on leave, but decided that we just could not afford them at that moment."

The Marquis thought he could understand that.

If Lady Windell required specialists from London, they always charged exorbitant sums for having to travel to the country.

"Then I did the most stupid and most idiotic thing that anyone could do," Charles continued.

There was an unmistakable pain in his voice and the Marquis asked,

"What on earth was that?"

"I gambled with what little money we did possess," Charles answered, "and I have just learned that I have lost every penny of it!"

"Gambled?" the Marquis enquired. "On the gaming tables?"

"No, no, of course not!" Charles answered gruffly. "I am not such a fool as that!"

"Then tell me what you did, Charles."

"I am on compassionate leave at the moment and, because my father felt that I had done enough in helping with my mother, he told me to come up to London for a short stay and enjoy myself."

"That was sensible," the Marquis commented.

"I thought it was delightful," Charles explained, "especially as I had just become acquainted with a famous beauty who everyone in London is now talking about."

"Who can that be?" the Marquis enquired.

"You must have heard of her, Rupert, the Comtesse de Courché, who has taken all of London by storm."

"Oh, I know who you mean," the Marquis said. "I have read about her in every newspaper and judging by her pictures in the magazines she is an outstanding beauty."

"She is certainly that," Charles carried on. "But by listening to her I have made a complete and absolute fool of myself and I don't know what I can do about it."

"Tell me what you have done," the Marquis said sympathetically.

"I was with Yvonne when she opened a letter and told me with great delight that she had just made herself a veritable fortune."

"How could she have done so?" the Marquis asked.

"She has a good friend in Paris who is in touch with the Ruler of an Eastern country, who is secretly selling a great deal of its possessions and he wants a good slice of the cherry for himself personally."

"You can be very sure of that," the Marquis smiled. "It's what happens in most Eastern countries all the time."

"I know," Charles said, "but this one was disposing of oil as well as all the Oriental products that apparently have a fascination for those who live in the West."

"So what happened, Charles?"

The Marquis was trying to coax his friend along to the climax of his story.

"Yvonne told me that it was as safe as the Bank of England and persuaded me to give her money that she sent on to France. And then a Frenchman was responsible for passing it on to the Eastern Ruler."

The Marquis made a murmur, but did not interrupt the flow that was now gathering speed.

"She had made so much herself," Charles went on, "it had seemed such a gift from Heaven at this particular moment when my father was hard up and my mother was still under the specialists."

"So what did you do?"

"I gave the Comtesse all of twenty-five thousand pounds," Charles replied, "believing her when she claimed that it would be trebled or even quadrupled within a few weeks."

"And it has not happened?"

"The Ruler who was organising the whole thing has died," Charles added bluntly.

He put his hands up to his eyes as he spoke and the Marquis knew that he was fighting hard to keep control of himself.

"I suppose," he said, "there is no chance of you getting your money back."

"About as much chance as my flying to the moon," Charles groaned. "You know just what it is like in the East even better than I do. Money passes from hand to hand and each man takes something for himself. When anything like this happens, the last man to hold it puts it straight into his pocket."

The Marquis knew this to be very true.

"So you have lost twenty-five thousand pounds," he said, "and I presume that you gave it to your Comtesse in cash."

"I thought that was indeed rather strange," Charles admitted, "but she told me that it was the only way it could be paid to the East. As the whole thing was done secretly it would be a great mistake, she added, for me to have my name on a cheque or anything like that."

The Marquis had been listening very intently to the whole sorry tale.

Then he asked,

"When did this happen?"

"I gave her the money only a week ago," Charles said, "and so I was not expecting to hear anything for some time. But just yesterday, when I called to see Yvonne de Courché, she told me of the catastrophe."

"Was she upset?" the Marquis asked.

"She was very sympathetic and commiserated with me in every possible way. But she naturally did not offer to give me back what I had given her to send to Paris."

"To Paris?" the Marquis quizzed.

"It's a good friend she has there who is arranging everything," Charles said. "When he has the money in his hand, he has it conveyed somehow to the country involved and straight into the Ruler's hands. This means that no one else, as far as I know, has any idea of what is going on."

The Marquis was silent for a moment and then he observed,

"I don't like the sound of it, Charles, and what is more I am suspicious."

Charles looked at him in surprise.

"Suspicious," he queried, "of what?"

The Marquis hesitated for a moment.

"I think that the man in Paris may be the key to the whole story and I would like to know more about him."

"Then you will have to ask Yvonne de Courché," Charles said. "She just told me that she had this friend in Paris. I think that his name was Henri something. Let me think, Henri Monte, that's it. I don't have his address or anything like that."

There was silence and then the Marquis said,

"I am thinking the whole scenario out carefully and to be frank, Charles, every instinct in my body tells me that there is something very fishy about the whole operation."

"I expect you are right, Rupert, I was such a fool to believe it possible to get rich quick. The trouble is I dare not tell my father at this moment what I have done, but in a week or so there will be nothing in the bank to pay the wages, so he will have to know then."

The Marquis did not comment further.

And then, as a Steward went past, he told him to bring a bottle of champagne.

"It's very kind of you," Charles said. "We have nothing to celebrate except that I have undoubtedly won the prize of being the biggest fool of the year!"

"You have been taken in like a great many others older and wiser than you by the glamour and intrigue of the East."

The Marquis sighed before he added,

"I was always finding people in India who thought they had bought for a song something which was worth a million or two. They were invariably disappointed and the Indian went away rubbing his hands because he had pulled off the same trick at least a hundred times before."

"And I make it a hundred and one," Charles said bitterly.

The Steward brought the champagne.

Charles drank a glass of it down quickly as if he felt that without some stimulant he might collapse.

The Marquis only sipped at his glass before he said,

"What I am going to do, Charles, is to write you a cheque for two thousand pounds so that, at the moment, there will be no need for you to tell your father or to be short of ready money."

"You cannot do that!" Charles exclaimed.

"You can hardly refuse an old friend for giving you a helping hand," the Marquis pointed out. "What I intend to do is to find out a great deal more about this mysterious Ruler, who died at the most inconvenient moment and, of course, this beautiful lady who has persuaded you to invest your money so stupidly."

"It's not her fault," Charles insisted. "After all she had done very well by it."

"Or so she says," the Marquis muttered slowly.

"You are not suggesting, Rupert, that Yvonne could do anything quite so crooked. Why should she? She has practically every man in London on his knees in front of her and, if she really wants money, she would only have to ask for it."

"She might want a lot more than anyone would be prepared to give her," the Marquis commented. "Or she might well feel embarrassed as most decent women would be in taking money from a man."

Charles laughed.

"Most women in the *Beau Monde* would be only too happy to pick up anything that's going. If they lose at a game of cards, they expect you to pay. If they are short of a new fur or a horse, there is always a Cavalier standing by ready to oblige!"

The Marquis filled up his friend's glass with more champagne.

"What I want you to do," he said, "is to keep your mouth shut about this and don't tell anyone else what has happened."

"I have no intention of doing so," Charles said. "I am not in the least proud of the mess I have made."

"I am going to see if the mess is as bad as you have been told," the Marquis proposed. "But how would I get to know this ravishing beauty who, I understand, has captured so many English hearts?"

"Where are you going tonight?" Charles enquired.

"To Marlborough House," the Marquis replied. "I understand that His Royal Highness the Prince of Wales is giving a special party, which is why I have been invited."

"Then you could bet your last farthing that Yvonne will be there," Charles said. "The Prince is in love at the moment, as he has been for quite some years now, with the entrancing Daisy Brooke. But I am told confidentially that it is slightly on the wane and I would expect that Yvonne de Courché could well take her place."

The Marquis walked over to a writing table.

Drawing his cheque book from his pocket, he wrote out a cheque for two thousand pounds payable to 'Captain Charles Windell'.

Then he sat down again in the seat next to Charles and handed him the cheque.

"I ought not to take this, Rupert," he said. "You are far too kind. But, if it is humanly possible, I swear to you that I will pay every penny of it back."

"What we have to worry about at the moment," the Marquis persisted, "is your twenty-five thousand pounds and, although it may well be like looking for a needle in a haystack, I am going to try to find it for you."

"If anyone could work a miracle like that, it is you, Rupert. Men in the Regiment have been telling me about the extraordinary things you have been doing in India."

The Marquis frowned.

"What one does not want, in India or here, is people talking. I can assure you that more men lose their lives by careless gossip than they do with bullets."

"I realise that is true in India," Charles said, "but here it is impossible for people not to gossip and when they do they only believe what they want to believe."

"And that is too much," the Marquis said. "I tell you what we will do, Charles. We will have luncheon and, if we can sit at a table just by ourselves, I want you to tell me everything you know about the beautiful Comtesse de Courché and by everything, I really do mean *everything*."

"Which to tell you the truth," Charles answered, "is very little. She suddenly appeared on the scene and took

London by storm. We learned that she was French and the Comte de Courché is conveniently dead."

"There must be a great deal more to know if one can find the right key to the safe," the Marquis suggested.

Charles laughed.

"You know the answer to that, Rupert, and no one could provide it better than you."

The Marquis's eyes twinkled.

"I was thinking the same," he murmured.

*

Zela was allowed to work in the library during the afternoon she arrived sorting out the pile of invitations that the Comtesse had received.

Then she was told that a room had been prepared for her office in another part of the house and it was very different from the library.

It was a small room not far from the pantry and she suspected that it had in the past been used as a bedroom for the butler or alternatively for a footman when on duty.

The walls were all bare and there was just the one window that overlooked the back of the house. There was no fireplace and it would be very cold for anyone who had to use it in the winter months.

Zela was provided with a writing desk that had seen better days and there was a cupboard containing shelves in which papers could be kept.

There were two hard chairs in the room to begin with, but the redoubtable Hannah found her a comfortable armchair in the attic and it would at least be there if Zela ever had the time to sit in it.

As soon as she had started work for the Comtesse, she found that the footman had been right.

She was on the run day and night.

There were letters and invitations that seemed to increase day by day and there were hundreds of things that the Comtesse wanted done that were the secretary's job.

There were French newspapers and magazines that were hard to find and they could not be ordered from the same shop that produced the English newspapers.

If a book was mentioned at a dinner party and then people were talking about it, the Comtesse would want it immediately.

Actually Zela enjoyed shopping and she found that it was more invigorating than sitting at her desk writing letters of acceptance or refusal. And it was better than having to pay a large amount of bills.

The Comtesse did everything in a grand way.

Because she was French she not only expected the very best food, she also demanded the best wine whatever the price.

'She must be very rich,' Zela decided and this was after she had only spent twenty-four hours in the house.

Then it struck her that the Comtesse was not only making herself famous because she was a beauty, but she wanted people to know that she was a rich widow.

Three days after Zela had arrived at the house she was struggling to keep her head above water.

At six o'clock in the evening the Comtesse sent for her after Zela had spent a long day shopping, answering letters and paying bills.

In fact she did not have a moment's rest from the time she had got up in the morning.

It was the butler, Dobson, who came to tell her that the Comtesse wanted to see her in her boudoir.

Zela sighed and said,

"There is no rest for the wicked!"

"Or for the good in this house," Dobson replied a bit cynically.

"What do you think she wants?" Zela asked as she put on her shoes.

"I've no idea," Dobson replied, "unless she wants you to go up to the moon and bring her down somethin' she had not thought of before!"

Zela laughed.

She found Dobson very amusing in a dry way.

As she took her meals in the housekeeper's room, she ate with Dobson and Hannah and, if there had been a lady's maid, she would have been included and it was also correct for the cook to eat with them.

The cook, however, was Dobson's wife and she said that she had no time to leave the kitchen.

This meant that Zela was alone with Dobson and Hannah and she found what they told her very interesting.

So far she had been careful not to seem too curious.

As she walked to the Comtesse's boudoir, she was wondering what her Mistress would require now or maybe she might easily have done something wrong unknowingly.

The Comtesse, looking exquisitely elegant in a very expensive and becoming negligee, was lying on the sofa.

When Zela came into the room, she called out

"I want to talk to you, Miss Lane. Shut the door!"

Zela did as she was told and then went to the sofa.

To her surprise the Comtesse said,

"Sit down and I want you to listen attentively to what I have to say."

"I am doing that, *madame*," Zela replied.

"I will be returning late tonight," she began, "with a gentleman called Lord Grandon of Neverton."

Zela's eyes widened, but she did not speak.

She knew who Lord Grandon was because he was a friend of her father's, who had often spoken about him and he was a man of about fifty-five and extremely rich.

He owned an ancestral home that was filled with magnificent pictures as well as priceless treasures that were often mentioned in the newspapers.

"I am dining tonight, as, of course, you will know," the Comtesse continued, "at Marlborough House with His Royal Highness the Prince of Wales."

Zela had answered the invitation and already knew about it.

"Now what I have to tell you," the Comtesse went on, "is in the strictest confidence and you must swear to me that you will not breathe a word of it to anyone."

"I can assure you, *madame*, that I am not a gossip," Zela replied. "Anything you tell me is safe, I will promise you."

"I hope that's true," the Comtesse muttered.

There was a pause and then she carried on,

"Because Lord Grandon is a close friend of mine he is lending me to wear tonight what is left of the necklace once owned by Queen Marie Antoinette of France."

Before Zela could make any remark the Comtesse said sharply,

"I suppose you are educated enough to remember the story of the diamond necklace which did so much harm to poor Queen Marie Antoinette?"

"Yes, indeed I know the story well, *madame*."

"But then do you know that what was left of the necklace eventually came to England," the Comtesse said, "and is now in the possession of Lord Grandon?"

"I did not know that," Zela answered. "But I have heard of the many treasures in his home at Neverton."

"What concerns me is that I am going to wear the necklace tonight at His Royal Highness's party."

Zela was listening to her and wondering what all this could be leading up to.

"Now what I am telling you," the Comtesse went on, "is that the last time I wore this necklace I dislodged one of the smaller diamonds in the clasp. It caught on my dress and I was so distressed at having been so clumsy that, when I handed it back to his Lordship, I did not tell him what I had done."

She gave a deep sigh before continuing,

"Luckily he has not yet noticed what has happened. Therefore tonight is my opportunity to replace the stone, which is quite a small one, and I don't have to tell him how careless I was."

"I do understand, *madame*," Zela murmured, "that it would be somewhat embarrassing."

"Very embarrassing," she agreed. "Therefore you will have to help me."

Zela wondered how, but she did not say anything.

"I have arranged," the Comtesse said, "that a man will come here at exactly eleven-thirty tonight and you will answer the front door to him."

A question trembled on Zela's lips, but she did not say a word.

"You will take him quickly upstairs and show him into this room," the Countess carried on.

"But surely," Zela said, "Dobson or the footman will hear the bell ring."

"The man will not ring the bell," the Countess said sharply. "He will knock on the door gently, you will open it and take him upstairs. No one else in the house will have the slightest idea that he is here. Do you follow me?"

"Yes, of course, *madame*," Zela replied.

"When I come back from Marlborough House and Lord Grandon will be with me," the Comtesse said, "we will go upstairs and I will take off the necklace, place it in its special case and put it outside the door of my bedroom."

She paused as if to be sure that Zela was listening before adding,

"As I don't want to let Lord Grandon see me do it," the Comtesse continued, "it will be done very quickly and I will lock the door, which will be my reason for going to it in the first place. Do you understand?"

"Yes, I understand," Zela said again.

"You will pick up the necklace in its case and take it to the man in my boudoir," the Comtesse went on. "He will repair it as we have arranged and then an hour later you will collect the case from him. Then you will put it back outside the door you took it from. Do you follow?"

"Yes, I follow," Zela replied.

"Then you will escort the man downstairs and let him out of the front door. After that you can go to bed."

The Comtesse stopped for breath before adding,

"Now whatever you do, don't make any mistakes otherwise I shall have to explain to his Lordship that I had damaged his precious necklace. In which case it will be very unlikely that he will ever lend it to me again."

"I will do exactly as you have told me, *madame*."

"I shall be very angry if anything goes wrong," the Comtesse snapped.

"Then I shall make sure that it all happens exactly as you have ordered, *madame*."

She rose from her chair and waited for a moment in case the Comtesse had anything further to say.

As she was silent, Zela then went from the room.

She recalled all too well the story of the necklace that had done so much harm to the poor French Queen. She had first read it at home with her Governess and she had been very sorry for the unhappy Marie Antoinette.

Her life at the age of thirty-six had ended on the guillotine and the infamous necklace had been the most audacious swindle in French history.

A Frenchwoman called Jeanne de la Motte claimed to be the direct descendant of King Henry II of France, the last of the Valois Kings.

She was totally unscrupulous and somehow she had managed to ingratiate herself into the Palace of Versailles.

She was pushy and ambitious and so was Cardinal Rohan, who had annoyed the Queen for some reason and she had not spoken to him for nine years.

Jeanne learned that the Cardinal's greatest ambition was to be acknowledged by Queen Marie Antoinette and she dreamed up a clever way of extorting money from him.

She told him that, because she was living in a part of the Palace of Versailles, she was a close friend of the Queen's. In fact she could persuade Her Majesty to show goodwill towards him.

Jeanne then went so far as to dress up a Baroness, whom she paid, to look like the Queen.

On a moonlight night she arranged it so that the Cardinal could see her nod towards him from her balcony.

Jeanne then discovered that a man called Bohmer, a jeweller to His Majesty, had one great desire. And that was to make the most opulent diamond necklace ever known.

He began collecting diamonds of the finest quality until he had six hundred and forty-seven brilliants.

First he made a choker of seventeen diamonds of five to eight carats and from these hung a three-wreathed festoon and pendants with a double row of diamonds. Also hanging from the necklace were four knotted tassels.

The whole piece of jewellery was enormous, but actually rather ugly.

Queen Marie Antoinette loved diamonds and had bought for herself a beautiful pair of earrings, but when the necklace was offered to her, she refused it and Bohmer was astonished and horrified.

He had spent so much money on the necklace that it had not occurred to him that the Queen would not want it.

However he then showed the King his 'wonderful' necklace and Louis took it to his wife and suggested that he gave it to her as a present, but again the Queen refused it.

She thought it far too expensive and there were so many diamonds that it was an *embarras de richesse*.

Bohmer was in complete despair until Jeanne de la Motte came up with a very clever idea.

She managed to persuade Cardinal Rohan that the Queen really did want the necklace, but the King must not know and, if he would buy it for Her Majesty, she would gradually pay him back.

The Cardinal reckoned that he was at last being appreciated by the Royal Court and he did what Jeanne suggested. He paid out large sums of money believing that it was on the Queen's behalf and Jeanne wrote notes to him and signed them '*Marie Antoinette of France*.'

Finally Cardinal Rohan could pay no more and the appalling crookedness of Jeanne de la Motte came to light.

The Cardinal, however, was so closely involved in the plot that he was tried by Parliament where eventually by just twenty-six votes to twenty-three he was found not guilty of the charges against him.

Jeanne de la Motte was condemned to be branded with a 'V' for *voleuse* and imprisoned in the Saltpêtrière Hospital in Paris for the insane for life.

But she managed to escape to England two years later.

There she took revenge on the Queen by publishing her memoirs and two thousand copies were sold in English and five thousand in French.

"*With my dying breath,*" she wrote, "*I maintain that illicit relations existed between Cardinal Rohan and the Queen.*"

Even more damaging to the King and Queen were the scurrilous songs that originated in Paris after Jeanne de la Motte's trial. Hundreds of them were circulated and it was impossible to catch their authors who were mostly fly-by-night journalists.

The smear of the saga of the necklace on Queen Marie Antoinette contributed eventually to the downfall of the French Monarchy in the Revolution in 1789 with both the King and Queen losing their lives on the guillotine.

As Zela walked back to her office she thought that what was left of the necklace was evil.

In fact it was as dangerous as it had originally been when it was first made and it would be such bad luck to wear those diamonds.

She had no wish to touch it let alone clasp it round her neck and she was surprised that the Comtesse wanted to wear it.

At the same time she could understand that Lord Grandon found the necklace interesting. It was a unique addition to his already magnificent collection.

She sat down in the armchair in her office thinking what a nuisance it would be to have to sit up so late when she was so tired.

But she could only be grateful that the man who was repairing the necklace apparently only needed an hour to do his work. Even so the Comtesse and Lord Grandon might not return to the house until after midnight.

Then she would be very late indeed going to bed and would undoubtedly be extremely tired tomorrow.

She sighed.

So far she had found nothing that would be of the slightest help to her father.

It was now beginning to look as if she had made a mistake.

She had hoped that by being with the Comtesse she would be able to find some clue as to what had happened to his money.

'Maybe he will be more successful in Paris,' she thought to herself, 'while all that I am likely to get here is a headache!'

CHAPTER FOUR

The Marquis duly arrived at Marlborough House at precisely the time he had been invited.

He was not the first.

There were a number of carriages outside and many coming up the drive behind him.

He was admitted, as had happened to him before, by a Scottish ghillie resplendent in Highland dress.

Inside two scarlet-coated powdered footmen took his hat and evening cape from him.

They were then passed on to the Major Domo in a short red coat with a band of leather across his shoulders.

A page in a dark blue coat and black trousers next escorted him up to the first floor.

As he reached it, the Marquis had a fleeting glance at several maid-servants, all of them in neat uniforms with lace caps on their heads.

He knew that it was their job to make the Prince of Wales's residence as it was claimed to be – the 'best kept house in London'.

As was usual with the Prince's special friends, he was first shown into the sitting room. This was considered to be a special privilege before he would later join the rest of the party.

It was a room the Marquis knew well and admired. The walls were ornately panelled and the chairs and sofas were upholstered in leather of the same colour as the rich blue velvet curtains.

There was the Prince's writing desk, the gold key to which he always wore on his watch chain.

Opposite the door there was a large table covered with documents, newspapers and reference books, but most eye-catching of all were the china, bronzes, ornaments and endless framed photographs placed on the cabinets, ledges and side tables.

The Prince was standing in front of the fireplace talking to a very pretty woman who the Marquis did not recognise.

When he was announced by the butler, the Prince turned to face him with what was almost a shout.

"Rupert!" he exclaimed. "It's delightful to see you. I thought you had forsaken London for ever."

Having made his formal Royal bow, the Marquis then clasped the Prince's outstretched hand.

"I have been in the country, Sire," he said, "trying to put to right all the matters that were neglected while I was in India."

"I want to talk to you about what you did there," the Prince said. "I hear from Cross that we owe you a great debt of gratitude."

Viscount Cross was the Secretary of State for India and the Marquis thought privately that he should keep his mouth shut.

Aloud he replied,

"Your Royal Highness is very gracious, but I have so much to catch up on in the Social world that I need your help."

The Prince obviously thought that this was a joke and laughed.

"What I am doing for you tonight," he said, "is to introduce you to all the new beauties, but, of course, you have missed some which have come and gone whilst you have been away."

"I must very certainly make sure of not losing any more," the Marquis remarked.

More guests were announced and he talked to them until the Prince said that they should now join the rest of the party downstairs.

Princess Alexandra had been receiving their other guests and the Prince led the way to a large room which had been emptied of furniture.

This told the Marquis that there would be dancing after dinner that would usually happen at the larger more formal dinners at Marlborough House while at the smaller evenings whist tables were set up after dinner.

But as the Marquis knew even the smaller evenings were far from conventional and they seldom ended before dawn.

He recalled parties when the younger gentlemen amused the company by tobogganing down the stairs on trays and there had been spirited battles with soda siphons and inevitably there was a profusion of practical jokes.

He had managed to avoid them, but there had been soapsuds on one man's pudding instead of whipped cream and another joke was on one who was known to drink and he discovered a foul-tasting medicine in his glass instead of wine!

Now the Prince of Wales was older and indeed so were most of his friends, the Marquis felt, gazing around the room.

Then the stentorian voice of the butler was heard to announce,

"The Comtesse de Courché."

This was who the Marquis was waiting for.

He turned sharply to see, as he expected, a vision coming through the doorway.

She certainly, he thought, deserved the praise she had received.

She was undoubtedly an outstanding beauty and her dark hair glittered with jewels.

And round her neck was a necklace of enormous diamonds.

The Marquis thought vaguely that it had a famous history, but for the moment he could not remember what it was.

As the Comtesse moved forward to curtsey very gracefully to the Prince, Lord Grandon of Neverton was announced.

The Marquis then remembered meeting him several times when he had been with his father and he had been told that he had the best private collection of pictures in the country.

Now the Prince was talking to the Comtesse.

He was clearly paying her the fulsome compliments at which he was an expert.

Cleverly, so that no one noticed what he was doing, the Marquis edged his way until he was close to the Prince, who was saying in his deep voice,

"You look more beautiful every time I see you, my dear. I am quite certain that you have a magic spell that no other woman has yet discovered."

The Comtesse gave a soft laugh.

"I only wish, Sire, that was the truth," she said. "If I did have, I would, of course, share it with Your Royal Highness."

"I only hope," the Prince said, "that you will share other things with me as well!"

The Comtesse gave him a provocative glance.

It was then that the Prince became aware that the Marquis was standing near him.

"What I will do," he said to the Comtesse, "is to introduce you to one of the most delightful of my friends, who has been away from London for far too long."

He paused to beam at her before continuing,

"His name is the Marquis of Buckwood and I am quite certain that he has already heard of your beauty and there is no need for me to inform him of your name."

"No need at all," the Marquis said. "I can only say that the stories I have heard were not exaggerated and in reality your beauty far exceeds all that has been related to me."

The Comtesse smiled and held out her hand and the Marquis bent over it in the French fashion.

"I have also heard about you," she said. "But they were mostly complaints because you were neglecting your friends who missed you when you were away for so long."

"My duty kept me out of the country," the Marquis replied. "But now I have been able to return I can only ask you to be kind to someone who has been left out in the cold and realises how much he has missed."

The Comtesse laughed.

"I am sure it has not been as bad as all that. At the same time I have a feeling that you will soon catch up with the Social world and there will be many eager teachers to show you how."

"Now you are being unkind," he protested, "when that is the position I have asked *you* to undertake."

The Comtesse seemed to hesitate for a moment.

Then she looked up into the Marquis's eyes with a provocative expression in her own.

It was one he knew only too well.

"I can but try to help you," she murmured softly.

The Marquis was seated at dinner between two old friends and they vied with each other in telling him the gossip and scandal of Mayfair.

It did not prove difficult for him to manoeuvre the conversation round to the Comtesse, who was at the other end of the table.

"Do tell me who is the new and latest great beauty in London?" he asked.

"You can see her quite clearly," the lady on his left answered. "We are all grinding our teeth and biting our fingernails, but we have to admit that in this battle France is definitely the winner."

"I would not go as far as to say that," the Marquis replied. "Englishmen have always preferred blondes."

The lady laughed.

"Few would agree with you at the moment, but then because she is here tonight I rather suspect that His Royal Highness could be enamoured."

The Marquis raised his eyebrows,

But he did not pursue that particular subject.

Then there was dancing after dinner was over and he managed rather skilfully, he thought, to have his second dance with the Comtesse.

She had danced the first with Lord Grandon. This was correct as she had come with him.

She had in point of fact been hoping that the Prince of Wales would ask her for the next waltz.

However, he was still talking to the very attractive Duchess who had sat on his right at dinner.

So the Comtesse accepted the Marquis's invitation and they moved onto the dance floor.

He was an exceptional dancer just as he was an outstanding rider and had been the winner of a number of races when he was at Oxford University.

The Comtesse seemed to float in his arms.

Then the Marquis said to her,

"There is so much I want to know about you, but I don't know where to begin."

"It sounds as if it will take some time," she replied rather provocatively

"It will indeed," the Marquis replied. "So when may I call on you?"

"I do have an appointment for luncheon tomorrow," the Comtesse said, "and several engagements later in the afternoon."

"And what about dinner?" the Marquis questioned.

"I am free," the Comtesse replied, "but I think if we want to talk seriously about ourselves it would be easier if you dined with me than if I dined with you."

"I would be very honoured to be your guest," the Marquis smiled.

"Then come to me at eight o'clock," she said. "Do you know where I live?"

"As it happens by a remarkable coincidence," the Marquis replied, "I live exactly opposite you on the other side of Berkeley Square."

The Comtesse laughed and it was indeed a very pretty sound.

"That is something I did not expect."

"My family have been there for nearly a hundred years," the Marquis remarked.

She laughed again before she admitted,

"I am only an interloper slipping in from another country just to have a look at all the excitement and gaiety of the *Beau Monde* that I have heard so much about."

"And it has accepted you at once with open arms," the Marquis then observed. "Everyone including His Royal Highness has told me that there is no other beauty to touch you."

"I only hope that is true," the Comtesse said. "But you shall tell me what you really think after we have dined together tomorrow night."

"I shall be counting the hours," the Marquis replied.

He did not have a chance for any more intimate conversation with the Comtesse as the Prince claimed her for the next dance.

After that he took her round Marlborough House and they were away for so long that when they did return some of the guests were already leaving.

The Marquis, however, did have a last word.

"You will not forget tomorrow what you promised me tonight," he smiled.

"I shall be looking forward to our meeting," the Comtesse said. "I feel that we have a great deal to say to each other."

"It's not only words that are important."

"That is something I am sure you will explain to me very eloquently," the Comtesse answered.

There was a suggestive twist to her red lips and the expression in her eyes spoke volumes.

As she turned away, the Marquis told himself that it had been easier than he had expected.

It was, however, very lucky that he should have met her in such grand surroundings and whatever she had heard about him from the Prince of Wales would undoubtedly have been complimentary.

Lord Grandon then took the Comtesse away.

The Marquis stayed on at the party for a short while as the Prince insisted that he should.

He told the Marquis that he must have luncheon with him tomorrow so that he could tell him about India and his opinion on recent events in the Subcontinent.

"I hear things are very difficult out there, Rupert," he said, "but Lord Lansdowne is, I expect, managing very well."

"The Viceroy has done his best to improve the local conditions considerably," the Marquis replied, "and I will tell you, Sire, all about it tomorrow."

He spoke quickly as he was feeling half-afraid that the Prince might ask him something about his work in *The Great Game*.

The Marquis was determined not to speak about it except behind closed doors and he knew only too well how gossip flew on the air in London.

Those who chattered away lightly had no idea how many spies the Russians operated in England and indeed in all parts of the world.

It would not have surprised the Marquis if he had been told that one of the Prince's guests tonight would be relaying anything that was said to the Russian Embassy.

From the Russian Embassy it would go straight to St. Petersburg and St. Petersburg would use it as they used other information as a weapon to strike at India with.

The Marquis reached his house in Berkeley Square and thought with a feeling of satisfaction that the evening had been a success.

He had managed to meet and make contact with the Comtesse de Courché far quicker than he had hoped.

He could well understand Charles being infatuated by her, but he was still finding it difficult to think why she should cheat him out of twenty-five thousand pounds.

She certainly appeared to have no need for money.

The opulent diamonds round her neck were almost blinding and there were other valuable jewels in her hair and on her wrists.

She had also rented a house opposite his, which he had heard was very expensive. It had been let to various people simply because its owner had fallen on hard times.

He knew the house well having been entertained there a number of occasions and it was most certainly the right backdrop for someone as beautiful as the Comtesse.

He wondered who at the moment was receiving her favours and then he realised that it must be Lord Grandon.

But he did not often come to London and therefore the Marquis decided that his Lordship must have received a very personal invitation for this particular evening.

'I cannot believe,' the Marquis thought with a faint smile on his lips, 'that Grandon is adding her permanently to his collection!'

*

Zela was asleep and dreaming when she was woken by a bell ringing over her head.

This meant that the Comtesse was home.

When she looked at the clock, she saw that it was half past twelve.

She put on her dressing gown and then she opened her door very quietly.

The house was completely silent.

She knew that the Comtesse would be in her room as she had told her.

At eleven o'clock she had been downstairs waiting for a knock on the front door.

As was usual all the lights in the hall were turned down with the exception of one and there was no sign of any of the servants.

In most houses, as Zela knew only too well, there was always a night footman in the hall. He sat and slept in a large padded chair and he was there to open and close the door whenever it was required.

There was a chair in the hall, but on the Comtesse's orders the footman slept on the top floor.

Zela had hoped that she would be able to read and had taken a book with her.

She had sat in the little morning room, which was next to the front door. It was very seldom used except by visitors who had to wait when the Comtesse was engaged.

She found, however, because it had been a long day that her eyes were tired.

She therefore put her feet on the sofa and thought about what had happened since she had arrived in London.

She had been busy for every moment of the day, but she had found nothing that would be of any help to her father than she had when she arrived.

Even to think about the mess they were in made her depressed.

She was then relieved when she heard the muffled knock on the door and she hurried to open it.

A small dark man slipped in when she had the door only half open.

In the faint light she saw that he was a Frenchman and he was carrying a case in one hand.

Although there was no one to overhear her, Zela said in a whisper,

"Follow me upstairs."

She went ahead of him and led the way into the boudoir.

There was a light burning on the table in the centre of the room. The Frenchman went to it and put his case down on the table.

"Is there anything you want?" Zela asked in her normal voice.

"*Non merci, mademoiselle*," the Frenchman replied speaking in his own language.

He then carried on in French,

"Madame le Comtesse has told me that you would bring me the necklace when she returned. Do you think she will be very late?"

"I am afraid so," Zela replied.

The Frenchman shrugged his shoulders as if it was what he expected.

He seemed rather small and somewhat pathetic and he obviously had a long and tedious wait in front of him.

"Would you like something to drink?" Zela asked him.

The Frenchman's eyes brightened.

"*Merci bien, mademoiselle*," he said, "that would be very pleasant."

Zela smiled at him and went downstairs.

The Comtesse had not told her to provide any food or drink for the man and she knew that she could not go to the kitchen.

If she did, there would be questions asked in the morning as to what had been taken and why.

In the drawing room there was a table in one corner on which there was a tray of drinks and they were always ready should any gentlemen require one.

If there was anyone invited for dinner, there was champagne in a cooler. Otherwise there were decanters filled with different wines.

Zela inspected them for the first time and there was one decanter that she thought contained port, while another held sherry and a third brandy.

She hesitated and then poured out a glass of port and carried it upstairs.

The Frenchman was profuse in his thanks and when she left him he said,

"*Merci mademoiselle, vous étès très bonne et très belle.*"

Zela laughed at this compliment and replied,

"*Merci monsieur,*" before she went out of the room closing the door.

Now she was quite sure that there would be a long wait before the Comtesse returned.

Because she knew that if she was asleep the bell would wake her, she climbed into bed.

She must have fallen asleep almost instantly.

When she woke, she was half-afraid that she dreamt that the bell was ringing and it might be part of her dream.

She then hurried along to the Comtesse's bedroom.

Now she could see that there was something lying on the floor outside the door and, as she picked it up, she heard voices inside.

She walked on tiptoe to the boudoir and opened the door and the Frenchman was inside.

He had obviously heard the Comtesse arriving and was waiting for the necklace.

It was in the black velvet case and, as Zela handed it over, she felt as if it was giving out vibrations of bad luck, as it had done all those years ago to the poor Queen Marie Antoinette of France.

Then, as the Frenchman took the case from her, she told herself that she was just being imaginative.

Without saying a word she then left the boudoir and went back to her own room.

She knew that whatever happened she must not fall asleep as she was yawning and her bed, small though it was, looked cosy and comfortable.

'If I fall asleep,' she told herself, 'I shall certainly get the sack early tomorrow morning. Then my journey to London and my hope of helping Papa will be finished.'

She went over to the window and, leaning out, she thought that the night air would keep her awake.

The window was at the front of the house and she could see below her the garden in the Square and the little ornamental Temple in the middle of it.

She knew that the owners of the houses in Berkeley Square all had a key that let them into the garden.

Dobson had one and she thought that, when she had time, she would go and sit under the trees.

So far there had hardly been time to breathe, let alone enjoy herself as if she was a lady of leisure.

She stood at the window for a long time and then she sat down at the dressing table and brushed her hair.

Her Nanny had always told her she must give her hair at least one hundred strokes a day, but she had been far too busy since she had came to London to do anything but comb it into place.

She must have glanced at the bedside clock half-a-dozen times.

Then she told herself that an hour had passed and the Frenchman would have finished repairing the necklace by now.

Because she was so anxious to get to bed she ran along the passage to the boudoir and then she remembered how quiet she must be.

She opened the door very slowly.

For a moment she could not see the Frenchman and thought that he must have gone.

Then she saw that the velvet case which contained the necklace was lying on the table and the Frenchman was at the far end of the room.

He was standing in front of the grand secretaire where the Comtesse wrote her letters and held something in his hands.

As Zela reached the table, she saw him put a thin box into the middle drawer of the secretaire.

She was wondering what it could be as he turned round and saw her.

He quickly closed the drawer and came back to the table.

"*C'est fini, mademoiselle,*" he said in a whisper.

Picking up the velvet box, which was lying on the table, he put it into Zela's hands.

"*Merci, monsieur,*" she answered.

She carried the box out of the room and placed it as the Comtesse had told her just outside her bedroom door.

The Frenchman had followed her from the boudoir and he was now walking along the passage.

He reached the top of the stairs and did not wait for Zela but hurried down into the hall.

She followed him and opened the front door.

"*Bonsoir, monsieur,*" she said.

"*Bonsoir, mademoiselle,*" he muttered and slipped out into the street.

Zela quickly closed the door.

She was about to bolt it and then she remembered that Lord Grandon was still upstairs. She had caught sight of his top hat on one of the chairs in the hall.

She then ran back to her own room.

She had done what she had been instructed to do and she did not want to think about Lord Grandon and the Comtesse together in the bedroom.

Because Zela was extremely well read she knew of course that Kings and Princes had mistresses.

Just occasionally she had heard people gossiping and it told her that secret liaisons or what the French called *affairs de coeur* took place in the Social world.

Her mother had never talked in front of her of such behaviour and Zela was not interested.

She always hoped that one day she would fall in love and she wanted to be as happy as her parents had been.

It had never occurred to her for one moment that she could be involved in anything like a liaison or that any friend of her father and mother would have one.

Now it struck her for the first time that her father must have been intimate with the Comtesse, just as she was at this moment being very intimate with Lord Grandon.

As Zela was so innocent, she had no idea exactly what they did.

If it was an expression of love, she supposed that they must find it very wonderful.

Then, because she was so tired, she did not want to think about it.

She had done what she was told to do.

The necklace that she knew was bad luck had been mended and that was all that concerned her and the sooner she could climb wearily into bed and go to sleep the better.

She pulled the curtains over her window and, taking off her dressing gown, got into bed. Then she blew out the candles.

Almost automatically, because it was the last thing she always did at night, she said a prayer.

It was a prayer that she had said every night since her father had left for Paris.

'Please dear God, help Papa so that he can get back some of the money he has lost that we need so desperately. Please God, *please*!'

Even as she murmured the last word of her prayer she fell asleep.

*

The Marquis arrived back at Buckwood House in Berkeley Square.

He thanked his coachman and he drove off.

Instead of opening the door with his key he thought that he would go into the garden as he needed some fresh air.

It was a warm balmy night, but it had been, he thought, particularly airless in Marlborough House and, as he had been in the country for so long, he felt it hard to breathe.

He did have not the special key to the garden with him.

Yet he was very athletic and it was an asset that had served him well when he had been in India. He therefore vaulted over the iron fence that surrounded the garden.

Then, putting his hat and cape down under a tree, he walked over the smooth grass.

He wished that he was back in the country and then he could go down to the lake, which he usually did in the evening, and there he would watch the swans and the ducks to his heart's content.

If it was moonlight like tonight, the water would be turned to silver. There would be something mysterious and magical about it which he had enjoyed all his life.

His mother had read him Fairytales when he was a very small boy and he believed fervently that there were fairies and goblins in the woods round Buckwood Park.

If there were ghosts in the house, they were most certainly his ancestors and, having lived at Buckwood Park for centuries, they could not bear to leave it.

It was India which had made the Marquis aware that the world could be a very dangerous and evil place and there were people in it who were undoubtedly driven by the Devil to make others suffer appallingly.

He had been forced to kill while he was in *The Great Game*.

His victims were all men who had done immense harm and in almost every case they had caused the death of a great number of innocent people.

That they had died by his hands did not disturb the Marquis as much as he expected and anyway, being in the Army, he knew that he would be forced to kill an enemy or be killed himself.

When it happened he had felt glad that so much evil had been taken from the world.

Yet at the same time he was happy now that he was no longer a soldier.

The peace, beauty and calm of England had seemed to him like a miracle after the horrors he had encountered in India.

He had so very nearly lost his life to an enemy who would use every underhand and inhuman trick they could to pillage and destroy.

Now the moonlight was shining through the trees in Berkeley Square and making little patterns of light on the grass.

The Marquis asked himself if anyone as beautiful as the Comtesse de Courché could do anything as deceitful and unpleasant as to steal so much money from someone like Charles.

He could understand why Charles wanted to believe her.

She had told him that the Ruler in the East had died or been killed at an unfortunate moment and yet somehow to the Marquis the story did not ring true.

It was not only what he had heard, his instinct had saved his life dozens of times when he had been in India.

He had known when his men were going up to the North-West Frontier before they arrived there that they would have a hard and difficult time and a number of them would lose their lives.

And so that same instinct now told him that the Comtesse was not what she appeared to be.

'I must be wrong,' the Marquis said to himself as he walked over the well-manicured grass.

But his instinct told him indisputably that there was a great deal more about the Comtesse that did not meet the eye.

Without meaning to he found that he had walked from his side of Berkeley Square to the other.

Then, as he gazed at No, 18, which was where the Comtesse was staying, he saw the door open.

To his surprise a small man slipped out.

It was certainly not anyone who would be visiting the Comtesse and the Marquis thought for a moment that it must be a burglar.

Then, as the man, holding a case, walked without hurrying along the pavement towards the end of Berkeley Square, he thought that no burglar would be so composed.

Also the man had made no effort to shut the door behind him and so someone must have let him out.

It seemed to the Marquis rather strange, but at the same time it was not his business.

Whoever the small man was he could have nothing to do with Charles.

The Marquis turned round to walk back to his own house.

'Tomorrow I will have to find out where Charles's money went,' he told himself, 'and if it really is completely lost.'

He had a strong feeling, and this was strange too, that the Comtesse would be very evasive and it would not be easy for him to obtain the information he required.

Then he recalled that he had dealt with the twisting, unscrupulous and cunning men of the East.

And he should therefore be able to deal with one Frenchwoman.

The Marquis left the garden the same way as he had entered it by vaulting over the iron railings.

He let himself into his house and went upstairs to his bedroom. He did not ring for his valet as his father would have done.

He undressed himself and threw his clothes onto a chair and then climbed into bed.

He was tired, but he had enjoyed the evening and was looking forward to having luncheon with the Prince of Wales.

For dinner he would be with the Comtesse and it was there, he told himself, that he would have to be very astute.

It just seemed impossible that she could be doing anything so cruel as to impoverish someone like Charles.

To the Marquis Charles had always been one of his closest and nicest friends and he could never imagine him deliberately hurting anyone, just as he had a gentle hand for a horse and was, as the Marquis well knew, loved by everyone on his father's estate.

He had often stayed with Charles as a boy and had thought that, if one day he owned a village or a farm, he too would be friendly with his people and they would look to him for understanding and, of course, for protection.

Now so unexpectedly because of his brother's death he owned a dozen villages and many acres of land.

And he was the owner of so many farms that he had not yet troubled to count them all.

'I will have to make them trust me and I hope that one day they will love me,' the Marquis thought before he fell asleep.

CHAPTER FIVE

Zela had a difficult morning coping with the large number of invitations that had arrived for the Comtesse.

There were some personal letters as well and her instructions were that, when she realised on the opening of an envelope that the letter was personal, she was not to read it and take it up to the Comtesse.

Zela went upstairs three times with three letters and this meant a wait while the Comtesse read them.

If Madame did not care to reply herself, Zela had to write down what she was to say.

The last envelope in the pile contained, when Zela opened it, another personal letter.

As she did not want to go upstairs for the fourth time, she read it.

She decided that, if it was not important, she would keep it until the evening when the Comtesse usually signed her letters.

When Zela read the first few lines, she stiffened.

It was a letter from a man who had apparently lost his money in the same way that her father had done.

He had written in the vague hope that the Comtesse would find that some of the money he had given her was left.

Or he hoped that it had not yet been sent off to the East.

It was a very pathetic letter.

Zela felt desperately sorry for Mr. Steven Howe, the man who had written it.

Once again the horror of what had happened to her father swept over her.

'I really must find out exactly what happens to all this money,' she thought. 'I cannot believe that it is all lost so quickly. Surely the Comtesse, or the man who had been handling it, could appeal to the heir who will now be ruling in the Eastern country whose name we have not even been told.'

She then put Mr. Steven Howe's letter back into the envelope.

She decided that she would wait until the Comtesse was in a good mood and perhaps then she could persuade her to help him.

'She must be so rich to live like this,' she thought. 'Even if she gave him a hundred pounds it would be better than nothing.'

She was still thinking about it when the Comtesse sent for her. It was just as she was leaving the house to go out to luncheon.

"I want a pair of new gloves to wear tomorrow," she said. "And also another pair of long white kids for the evening. As the shop is not too far away, you can walk there and buy me as well some of the face powder I always use from the chemist."

She was walking through the hall as she was giving these orders and was still doing so as she stepped into her carriage.

The footman closed the door behind her.

As she drove away, Zela sighed to Dobson,

"I really cannot think how I am to get all the letters written and go shopping as well."

"She always wants the impossible," Dobson said. "Go and have your lunch, miss, and that'll make you feel a lot better."

Zela thought that she was indeed rather hungry and went up to the housekeeper's room to find that Hannah was already there.

As soon as Zela sat down at the table, one of the footmen brought in the dishes and put them down on the table.

"I'd suppose that you've 'ad a real busy mornin'," Hannah began.

"So busy," Zela replied, "that I am now beginning to think that what is needed here is a machine and not a secretary!"

"That'll be the day for sure," Hannah countered and then they both laughed.

Dobson came up a few minutes later and sat down at the end of the table.

"I've got news for you two," he said. "Who do you think's comin' to dinner tonight?"

"I've no idea," Hannah replied, "unless it be the Prince of Wales himself."

"Not as grand as that," Dobson carried on, "but more excitin'."

"For us or 'er?" Hannah asked pertly.

"It's someone who might have stepped straight out of a story book," Dobson said. "And I'd rather it be him than any King or Prince in the whole world."

Both Hannah and Zela looked at him in surprise.

"Who can it be?" Zela enquired. "Do we really have to guess?"

"No, I won't let you do that, because you ain't clever enough," Dobson answered. "It be the Marquis of Buckwood."

Zela started because she knew very well who the Marquis of Buckwood was.

Hannah, however, asked,

"Why's 'e so important I'd like to know?"

"I'll tell you," Dobson replied. "At the beginnin' of last year I were asked in a hurry if I'd go to help out at No. 10 Downing Street."

"To the Prime Minister!" Hannah exclaimed.

"Yes, that's right. His butler had fallen down and fractured his leg. As I were free, I then found myself in that Holy of Holies afore I could say 'Jack Robinson'."

"It must have been interestin'," Hannah murmured.

"It were hard work," Dobson said. "People comin' and goin' all day and Receptions almost every night."

He paused for a moment.

Then he added,

"One day I hears somethin' really interestin'."

"What was that?" Hannah asked.

"The Marquis of Salisbury, and he were the Prime Minister at the time, had the Viscount Cross to luncheon with him alone."

"Who is 'e?" Hannah enquired.

"He be the Secretary of State for India," Dobson replied. "And that's a country that's always intrigued me a good deal."

Zela was listening intently.

As if he appreciated her attention, Dobson said,

"I'd always thought I'd like to be an adventurer or an explorer, but listenin' to what I hears at that luncheon were somethin' I'll never forget."

"Do tell us what you heard," Zela quizzed him.

94

"After they had finished eatin', I puts the port and brandy on the table and then I leaves the room."

He smiled before he went on,

"That's what they thought. There were a screen in front of the pantry door to keep out the draught and believe it or not the door didn't shut too tight."

Zela laughed.

She realised that he had been eavesdropping on the Prime Minister's private conversation.

"So what did you hear?" she asked.

"I hears the Prime Minister sayin', 'tell me what's happenin' in India, my Lord. Is there any trouble?'"

"'Rather more than usual,' Viscount Cross replied, "but we owe a great deal of gratitude to Captain Rupert Wood.'

"'You were sayin' how extremely clever he was in *The Great Game*,' the Prime Minister said.

"'What he has done this time is truly amazing,' the Viscount replied. 'And I can only wish that more people at home knew exactly what those who fight in India manage to achieve for us. In fact in this case it was a miracle!'

"'Tell me about it,' the Prime Minister said."

Dobson paused for a moment to clear his throat before he continued,

"'There was trouble as usual up on the North-West Frontier,' the Viscount said, 'and no one realised that Fort Pontha was not sufficiently manned if there should be an assault of any kind!'

"The Prime Minister," Dobson remarked, "was, I thought, frownin' because he says quite harshly,

"'Surely that was very remiss. They must know by this time that the North-West Frontier must be held at all costs.'

"'The Viceroy is well aware of that,' the Viscount replied. 'But unfortunately because India is so big we are short of soldiers. It's difficult to keep every Fort alert not only against assault but infiltration.'

"'I am aware of that,' the Prime Minister said in a lofty voice."

Because Dobson stopped for a moment to draw breath, Zela said,

"Please go on, I am really interested."

"So be I," Dobson replied. "The Viscount says it were Captain Wood who discovered what them Russians were up to as he moved amongst the tribesmen disguised as a Holy Man. A 'Fakir' I thinks they calls it."

He mispronounced the word, but Zela knew what he meant.

"He finds out," Dobson went on, "that the Fort is goin' to be attacked with all them in it not expectin' any trouble. Them Russians had provided the tribesmen with weapons they'd never carried before and guns that could do a great amount of damage. In fact the Fort had little chance of resisting the bombardment."

"That be trouble!" Hannah exclaimed.

"The Viscount says," Dobson continued, "'the Fort would undoubtedly have fallen into the enemy's hands.'"

"'But you did say that Captain Wood managed to save it?' the Prime Minister asked.

"He spoke," Dobson said, "quietly as if he were afraid that after all the Fort had been taken."

"But it had not," Zela queried.

"Not when we had a man like Captain Wood to save us," Dobson replied.

He went on to describe just what Captain Wood had done.

Disguised as a tribesman he had walked a fantastic number of miles and climbed down the side of a mountain.

He warned the British that more soldiers must be sent to the Fort. At the same time he had learnt that those who were already on their way to the North-West Frontier would be ambushed before they reached it.

Entirely due to him the soldiers then approached the Fort from a different angle.

On their arrival outside the Fort they attacked the forces that the Russians were controlling before they were ready to make their own attack.

It resulted in the enemy being completely defeated, their weapons were taken from them and a large number of them were killed.

Due to Captain Wood deaths of the soldiers in the Fort were few and only a small number of the British were wounded.

As Dobson described it, his voice was excited and his eyes were shining.

Zela felt that she could visualise only too clearly what a triumph it had been.

She was particularly interested because her father had spoken so often about the Marquis of Buckwood and he had been distressed when he heard of his death.

She had learned that the second son had succeeded to the title as his elder brother was dead.

She thought perhaps she had met him when she was a child and she had no idea that now he was such a hero.

In fact Dobson was just saying,

"If I had my way, I'd give him the Victoria Cross. That's what he justly deserves."

"Then why can't he have it?" Hannah enquired at once.

"Don't you see," Dobson said, "that anythin' to do with *The Great Game* in India be so hush-hush I could have me head cut off for talkin' about it now."

He paused before he added,

"I expects it were a good thing that, as his father died, Captain Wood had to come home. Otherwise them Ruskies would have got him sooner or later."

"It makes me shudder to think of it," Hannah said. "A nasty lot they be and why should they want to take India from us, I'd like to know?"

"A very great number of people have asked that question," Dobson replied, "and from what I hears when I was at the Prime Minister's it be real excitin' for me to have his Lordship comin' here tonight."

"I'm sure it is," Hannah remarked. "I'm certain Mrs. Dobson'll cook him a right good dinner."

"I'll see to that," Dobson said. "He'll also have the best of the best from the cellar."

Zela was fascinated by what she had been hearing and she only wished that she could remember more about Rupert Wood.

It was indeed a long time ago since she had once been taken by her father to Buckwood Park. In fact now that she thought about it she could only have been seven or eight at the time.

Yet she could remember how magnificent it was and her father had often talked about the house and how much he admired it.

She wondered now that, as the Marquis had such fine possessions and must know every influential person in the country, why he was dining with the Comtesse.

Then suddenly the idea struck her.

"Surely," she said, "the Marquis of Buckwood is a very rich man and cannot want for anything."

Dobson shook his head.

"You can never be sure," he answered. "Things have been difficult for them big landowners the last year or so. I expects too that the new Marquis has been stuck for large death duties on his house and land."

"Do you really think he is short of money?" Zela asked.

"It wouldn't surprise me," Dobson said. "The last gentleman I were with acted just like he was a millionaire and when he died they finds he had so many debts he were on the verge of bankruptcy."

Zela was silent.

She was thinking of how awful it would be if the Marquis gave a great deal of his money to the Comtesse.

He might then find that he could not afford to live in his home, which was one of the most famous ancestral houses in the whole of England.

Now she thought back at what she had seen.

She had not realised at the time that it had been built by the famous Adam Brothers in about 1750 and it was a perfect piece of Palladian architecture.

She could remember her father talking about the beautiful pictures in the house and they were, of course, all entailed from father to son.

She could remember the lake and she had enjoyed more than anything seeing the swans and ducks swimming on it.

"Now what I thinks," Dobson was saying, "is that heroes like him should be appreciated by us as stays at home. They be fightin' enemies like the Russians and them Africans be always makin' trouble."

"I expects 'e'll have a statue put up to 'im sooner or later," Hannah commented.

"That'll do him a lot of good when he's under the sod," Dobson remarked.

He pushed back his chair and rose from the table.

"All I can do is to see that he has the best dinner and the best wine. That's what he deserves right enough."

"I'll most certainly take a peep over the banisters at 'im," Hannah said. "I expects, Miss Lane, you'll 'ave a good peep too."

Zela smiled but did not answer.

She was thinking to herself as she went back to her office that whatever happened tonight the Comtesse must not persuade the Marquis to give her money he could not afford.

Madame would promise to invest it with a Ruler, who was already dead, if he ever existed in the first place.

Zela wondered wildly how she could prevent him walking into what she guessed was a trap that had been set so successfully for others including her poor father.

She wondered if she should tell Dobson to warn him.

Then she knew that it was impossible.

If the Marquis was to be warned, it was something that she had to do herself.

*

The Marquis enjoyed his luncheon alone with the Prince of Wales.

He told him a great deal about India that he did not already know and he listened attentively to every word.

His mother, Queen Victoria, would not allow him to take any part in any way with the ruling of the British Empire and she forbade him even to see the despatches of the Foreign Office and he longed for information that other people did not have.

Because he had a good brain, it often occurred to the Marquis it was cruel that he was not allowed to use it and so it was not surprising that he wasted so much time flirting with beautiful women.

The doors of information were closed against him in the harshest way.

Everyone much admired the way that Her Majesty the Queen was promoting the ever-expanding Empire and in fact it had made Britain greater and stronger than she had ever been in the whole of history.

At the same time like many women she was very possessive.

It was wrong for her not to share her victories and her successes with her son and the Marquis well knew how much the Prince resented this.

He therefore told His Royal Highness a great deal more about *The Great Game* in India than he would have told anyone else and the Prince was unreservedly grateful.

"You have told me a great deal of all that I long to know," he said. "I only wish that it was in my power to thank you on behalf of the British Empire for what you have personally achieved so bravely."

"I don't want any thanks, Sire," he replied. "But I am extremely grateful for having had the chance to fight in any way against those marauding Russians. I am also very grateful to be alive!"

"Thank God you are!" the Prince exclaimed. "And now you are back with us again, we must make certain that you enjoy yourself."

"I am doing that already," the Marquis said. "First by seeing you, Sire, and then by dining tonight with a new beauty."

"The Comtesse?" the Prince enquired. "Well, you certainly work quickly! You only met her last night."

"I invited her to dinner on the off chance she would accept," the Marquis replied, "and believe it or not, Sire, she insisted that we dine together at her house."

The Prince chuckled.

"Much more convenient for walking upstairs, my boy!"

"It did just pass through my mind," the Marquis admitted with a little grin.

There was silence for a moment and then he asked,

"Do tell me, Sire, everything you know about her. After all I have only just met her for the first time."

"To tell you the truth I have asked that very same question," the Prince said. "And have not yet received an intelligent answer. She appeared very unexpectedly, she took London by storm and it is now the ambition of every young man like yourself to have dinner alone with her."

The Marquis laughed.

"The unknown and anticipation is always so much more exciting, I have found, than the reality."

"Now you are being a cynic," the Prince observed. "What I shall want to know is if she is as glamorous and scintillating as she looks."

"I am hopeful, Sire, that the answer will be in the affirmative," the Marquis answered.

The two men were laughing as they left the dining room.

And as the Marquis said goodbye to his host, the Prince said,

"Good luck and good hunting, Rupert. I wish that I was in your shoes."

With difficulty the Marquis prevented himself from saying,

'I am sure, Sire, you will be!'

He had a feeling that the Prince was almost jealous of him.

His Royal Highness had been ardently in love with Daisy Brooke for over eight years, but now the liaison was, as someone had said, paling a little.

The Marquis was not in the least surprised, as, of all the infatuations of the Prince of Wales, this one had lasted the longest.

It was whispered amongst his more personal friends that he was so much in love with Daisy Brooke that he thought of her almost as if she was his wife.

At the same time the Prince's behaviour towards Princess Alexandra could not be questioned. The country treated her as if she was a fairy doll on top of England's Christmas tree. Glittering with diamonds, she was blue-eyed, golden haired and very lovely!

The Prince appeared in public to think of her in the same way and he always treated her with deference.

However angry her lack of punctuality made him, he never spoke severely to her and she, in return, never criticised him to anyone.

Marvellously dressed, she was gracious, radiant and smiling and appeared neither to know nor to notice if there was anyone else of any consequence in her husband's life.

Her Royal Highness was coming through the front door just as the Marquis was leaving.

He thought how lovely she looked and the smile that she gave him was a genuine expression of delight.

"I am so glad that you are back with us, my Lord," she said. "Please do come to see us as often as you can. Edward does so enjoy having you with him."

The Marquis reflected that no one could be kinder or more thoughtful.

As he left, he thought that if he ever married, which he had no intention of doing at the moment, he hoped that his wife would be as magnanimous.

Equally he did not envy the Prince of Wales.

Moving from beauty to beauty and, having so little serious work to do, was bound to become boring.

'I would so much rather be myself,' the Marquis mused.

When his horses neared Berkeley Square, he was wondering just how he could help Charles.

Would tonight give him a clue as to how his friend had been robbed of such a large sum of money?

*

A clue was what Zela was seeking too.

She had spent a busy afternoon.

When the Comtesse did return from luncheon, she went to the drawing room, carrying all the letters that Zela had written for her.

The Comtesse was looking particularly attractive.

She was wearing a pink dress which was echoed by the ostrich feathers in her hat.

She signed all the letters that Zela handed to her one after the other and then she started to find fault with the arrangements of flowers in the room.

"Surely someone could have more sense than to put that large vase on the table by the window," she asked.

"I will move it," Zela offered. "Where, *madame*, would you like it put?"

She had it moved to several different places and finally she admitted that it was best where it had been put originally.

Then she said sharply,

"I am going up to rest before dinner. Kindly see that I am not disturbed. And tell Hannah I want my bath at seven o'clock."

"I will do that, *madame*," Zela replied.

She walked towards the door and, as she reached it, the Comtesse said,

"It seems to me that you have had very little to do today, Miss Lane. Therefore I have a long list of shopping for you for tomorrow morning. I am far too busy to have people idling about."

Zela did not answer.

She knew that, if the Comtesse was in one of her moods, it meant that she would complain about anything whatever it may be.

It would be no use saying that she had hardly had time to breathe all day.

Zela walked away from the drawing room and, as she did so, she had an idea that perhaps the Comtesse was annoyed with her because she was young.

She was also not as plain as many women were in her position. In fact the only women secretaries that Zela had ever seen had all been over forty.

'It does not seem,' she said to herself as she walked to her office, 'that I shall find anything here after all.'

She sighed and her thoughts continued,

'I suppose I might as well go back to the country. At least I shall have the horses to ride.'

Then she wondered if they would be able to keep the horses. It would be impossible if her father did not get back some of the money he had lost.

The idea was frightening.

As Zela then reached the door of her office, she was saying to herself,

'I have to find something! I have to!'

The day seemed to drag on.

Dobson came in and out because he was fussing about dinner.

"Come and see the way I've arranged the table," he said to Zela. "I've done it differently to what I usually does. If you don't like it, I'll change it back."

It was, however, a very pretty arrangement.

There were flowers round the candles and a silver bowl filled with white orchids.

"I think it's enchanting," Zela enthused.

"I hopes his Lordship notices it," Dobson replied. "Although I expect he has better at Buckwood Park at least for the moment."

The way he spoke the last words told Zela that he was worrying just in case his beloved hero was short of money.

If indeed he was, Zela thought, he might be very much shorter by the time this evening ended.

She was in her bedroom when Hannah came in to say,

"'E should be 'ere any minute. Ain't you comin' to have a look at 'im after all Mr. Dobson 'as told us about 'im?"

Zela that thought Hannah would be disappointed if she refused and so she walked with her to the top of the stairs.

She could not help feeling, as her father's daughter, that it was rather strange behaviour.

She had to peep round the corner to see a visitor arriving rather than receive him in the drawing room.

But, if it made Hannah happy, what did it matter?

And, as it happened Zela, *was* very interested.

Dobson opened the front door and the Marquis walked in while she was wondering if there was anything about him that she would remember.

What she had not expected was that he would be so good-looking.

He was over six foot tall with broad shoulders and he had very clear-cut English features and a high forehead which was a sign of a good brain.

As his house was on the other side of the Square, the Marquis was not wearing a tall hat or his evening cape.

He looked very smart and composed, Zela thought, in his evening clothes.

As he followed Dobson towards the study where the Comtesse was to receive him, he looked very much a hero.

"Now that's what I calls a man," Hannah said as the Marquis disappeared. "I'm sure that 'alf the women in England'll be runnin' after 'im. So no wonder Madame wanted to get 'er 'and in first!"

She hurried away to tidy the Comtesse's bedroom.

Zela was thinking furiously how she could warn the Marquis not to give the Comtesse any of his money.

She felt instinctively that, although the Comtesse was attracted to him as a man, she also needed something concrete from him, just as she had taken that huge sum of money from her father.

'Surely he cannot be such a fool as to trust her the very first evening he comes here?' she then asked herself angrily.

Yet she was frightened that he might actually do so.

She went and had a quick supper with Hannah in the housekeeper's room, but she could think of nothing but how she could warn the Marquis.

She had been told earlier that Dobson would not join them this evening as he had to see to the dinner.

Afterwards he and his wife would finish the best dishes in the kitchen when the Comtesse and the Marquis would go up to the drawing room on the first floor.

As Zela knew only too well that they only had to cross the passage to her bedroom.

She asked herself if that could really happen on what appeared to be such a short acquaintance and she did not like to think of the likely answer to her question.

She walked to her own bedroom.

Instead of undressing she went to the window and gazed out into Berkeley Square.

Everything that Dobson had said earlier about the Marquis kept repeating and repeating itself in her mind.

He was a hero.

He had saved a great many men from dying.

He had saved the Fort in India from the Russians and the Prime Minister was very grateful to him.

Yet one Frenchwoman, because she was beautiful, could do him immeasurable harm that the Russians had totally failed to do.

Zela looked at the clock and realised that it was now getting late.

It was after eleven o'clock.

On an impulse or rather because she just could not prevent herself she went downstairs.

She slipped into the little reception room which was on one side of the hall.

She left the door ajar and waited.

There was no light in the room and the hall was dimly lit as it always was in the evening.

On the Comtesse's strict orders Dobson and the footmen were in their own part of the house.

Zela sat down on the edge of a chair that was near the door.

If anyone was coming down the stairs she would see them.

She did not imagine that the Comtesse would come down with the Marquis.

If she did, then she would have had this long wait for nothing.

Otherwise she must think of what she would say quickly and quietly.

'I do hope he will not be very long,' she thought.

There was silence in the house with occasionally the sound of a carriage passing on the road outside.

*

The Marquis sat up and started to get out of bed.

"You are not leaving me!" the Comtesse exclaimed and put out her hand to stop him.

"It's getting late," the Marquis replied, "and I have an early appointment tomorrow at the War Office."

"But I want you to stay with me," the Comtesse said in a seductive voice. "You are a very wonderful lover, *mon brave*, and I want you with me."

The Marquis was, however, busily putting on his clothes.

He did so with the swiftness of a man who was used to looking after himself.

He thought as he tied his tie in front of the mirror that the Comtesse was very ardent, very exotic and very French and it was no less than he had expected.

He realised that so far he had learned nothing that he wanted to know.

Dinner had been excellent and the conversation had been witty, amusing and most entertaining.

He had realised when they had walked up the stairs towards the drawing room what she expected from him.

He had taken the Comtesse in his arms and she had melted against him with an expertise that made him think cynically of how often she must have done it before.

Her bedroom with the dimmed lights, the fragrance of flowers and the lace-edged pillows was exactly what he had forecast.

No man who could call himself a man could fail to respond to the Comtesse's ardent advances and she made the flame of passion burn brightly.

The Marquis was all she had expected and more.

She was well aware that all the women who looked for a man to delight them would be envious of her.

She had seen this last night at Marlborough House and the expression on many of the women's faces told her that they were wondering how soon they themselves could get the Marquis into their clutches.

Yet she had succeeded.

And now she was determined not to let him go.

"When shall I see you again, Rupert?" she asked him very softly.

It was a voice that made most men feel protective and that she was a weak little woman who had no husband to look after her.

"When will you be free?" the Marquis asked.

He was putting on his evening coat as he spoke.

"I have luncheon tomorrow," she said, "with Lord Grandon before he returns to the country. I have promised to let him escort me to the Duchess of Devonshire's dinner tomorrow night."

"I think I have been asked to that as well," the Marquis remarked, "so I shall see you there."

"That is not enough," the Comtesse purred. "I want to touch you and, of course, to kiss you."

The Marquis walked back to the bed.

"So what can we do about it?" he asked.

"Then we will have dinner the following night," the Comtesse suggested.

"Very well," he replied. "But this time you must dine with me. I would like you to see my house as perhaps I shall not have it for very long."

The Comtesse looked surprised.

"You are thinking of selling it? I thought you told me that your family had been there for a hundred years or more."

"They have, but, if something has to go, it will be better for it to be the house in London, which I seldom use, than anything in the country."

There was a little pause and then the Comtesse said,

"When I dine with you, I shall have something to tell you that I think will help you."

The Marquis now heard what he was expecting.

"I am not interested," he said, "in what I shall hear but what I shall see. You know how lovely you are."

He bent forward as he spoke and took her hand in his.

He kissed it and his lips lingered for a moment on the softness of her skin.

Then he said,

"Goodnight, Yvonne, and thank you."

Her fingers closed over his so that for the moment he could not leave.

"You will think of me," she murmured, "because I shall be thinking of you, *mon brave*."

111

She spoke to him in French which made it seem more intimate.

The Marquis kissed her hand again.

"Is it possible that I could think of anyone else?" he asked.

Then, as she still tried to hold onto him, he moved quickly across the room and opened the door.

"*Au revoir*, Yvonne," he called and was gone.

The Comtesse gave a little sigh and threw back her head against the pillows.

'He is mine!' she told herself. '*Mine!*'

The Marquis was hurrying down the stairs.

He reached the hall and was walking towards the front door.

Then to his astonishment someone came out of the room on the other side of it.

He could see that it was a woman who seemed very small and insubstantial in the dim light.

There were little flickers of gold in her hair and, as she raised her face to his, he saw that she was very young and surprisingly beautiful.

She came close to him and then she said in a voice that he could only just hear,

"Don't give Madame any of your money or you will lose it all."

Just for a moment the Marquis was silent.

He knew that this was what he had been waiting to hear.

In a very low voice he said,

"Meet me in ten minutes in the garden. I will leave the gate open for you."

Then he walked out of the door and Zela closed it behind him.

CHAPTER SIX

The Marquis walked slowly towards the gate into the garden of Berkeley Square.

He opened it with the special key he had brought with him, as he had felt that it would not be appropriate to vault the railings in his evening clothes.

He had, however, used his usual quickness of mind.

It could well be dangerous for this unknown girl to come to him directly he had left the Comtesse's house.

It was unlikely, but many of the women he usually left would watch him from the window as they hated him leaving them.

He left the gate unlocked and walked first under the trees as if he was heading for his own house.

Then he turned back and went to the little Temple in the centre of the garden.

He sat down on the bench inside and waited.

When he thought that the girl would be on her way, he rose and went outside the Temple.

He did not go far, just far enough that he could not be seen from the windows of the Comtesse's house.

A few minutes later he turned round to see Zela come hurrying towards him.

She had, before she left, gone very quietly into her office and had picked up the letter from Mr. Steven Howe that she had still not given to the Comtesse.

As she reached the Marquis, the moonlight was on his face and she thought again how handsome he was.

Dobson was so right in saying that he was a 'real live hero' and she was determined that he should not be ruined by greedy villains as her father had been.

The Marquis smiled at her.

"Come and sit down," he suggested quietly. "I feel that you have a great deal to tell me."

As they walked into the little Temple, Zela knew that this was not true.

She only wished that she could tell him where the money that her father and Mr. Steven Howe had lost had gone.

But all she could do now was to prevent any of the Marquis's following it.

They both sat down on the bench inside the Temple.

The Marquis was now thinking that the girl who had come to him out of the blue was not only very lovely but in every way a lady.

He had thought when she first appeared that she might be a servant, but now his instinct, as well as his eyes, told him that she was indeed well born.

He was also certain that she was well educated.

Because for the moment they were both silent, he said at last,

"You know that I am waiting eagerly to hear why you have been kind enough to prevent me from losing my money."

"I could not bear to think, after all you have done so bravely for our country," Zela began in a low voice, "that your money should be stolen from you as it has been from others."

"So how do you know about all this?" the Marquis asked her.

"I am the secretary to Madame la Comtesse," Zela replied, "and I want you to read this letter which came this morning."

She handed him the letter from Mr. Steven Howe.

As they were sitting in the shadows, the Marquis had to rise to his feet and go to the opening of the Temple to read it in the moonlight.

He turned first to see the signature and, when he did so, he exclaimed,

"But, of course, I know Steven Howe. He was at school with me."

Zela said nothing.

She felt it was actually wrong of her to show him a private letter, but she had been very moved by what the man had said.

And it seemed right to her that she should save the Marquis from suffering as her father was suffering.

The Marquis read the letter and then put it into his pocket.

Next, as he sat down beside her, he said,

"Why does it concern you so much that this should be happening to a very charming young man?"

"Because it has – also happened," Zela replied in a strained voice, "to – my father."

The Marquis looked at her in surprise.

And then he quizzed her,

"So are you trying to find out where the money has gone?"

Zela did not answer him for a moment and then she said,

115

"I am convinced, although I have no evidence, that the money did not go to the Ruler – who is now apparently dead."

She hesitated and then went on,

"That is what my father was told and also, as you have seen, the man who wrote this pleading letter."

"The Comtesse said the same thing to a good friend of mine," the Marquis replied, "which is exactly why I am so determined to learn the truth."

Zela clasped her hands together.

"Do you think you can do that? Oh, please do try, my Lord. If there is only a little money left, it would be better than losing so much."

"I can see that this means a great deal to you," the Marquis said. "But I think we should start at the beginning and firstly you should tell me your name."

"Zela – " she replied impulsively and then stopped.

She had made a mistake.

She thought then that it would be much wiser and certainly more sensible of her to give him the name that the Comtesse knew her by.

" – Lane," she finished.

The Marquis had noticed the pause between the two names.

Then he enquired,

"So, as your father has suffered at the Comtesse's hand, you have taken the position of her secretary without, I suspect, her knowing that you are your father's daughter."

Zela thought that this was very intelligent of him to have worked out her situation so quickly.

"Yes," she answered, "that is true, but I can only tell you that I have found nothing, absolutely nothing, to show where the money has gone or to prove that what the Comtesse has been saying is untrue."

"But like me you think that it is?" the Marquis said quietly.

"I am sure of it, my Lord. It is what my instinct tells me – but we must have proof."

There was such pain in her voice that the Marquis put out his hand and laid it gently on hers.

"Now listen," he said. "If we work together and if you help me as you have helped me already, I feel sure that between us we will be able to find out where this money has gone."

He drew in his breath before he added,

"God knows how many people have suffered like Steven Howe, your father and my friend, who is in utter and complete despair."

"I was so frightened," Zela said, "that you would be – added to the list."

"I might well have been, if I had not known before tonight how deeply one of my friends is suffering."

"So you would not have given her any of your own money?" Zela asked.

"If you are thinking of now regretting that you have been brave enough to warn me," the Marquis said, "I can only thank you from the bottom of my heart for doing so."

He thought that Zela looked surprised and her hand moved against his.

"I was working entirely in the dark," he continued. "But now I have you to help me and I feel that the Gods are on our side and we shall win this fight."

"I have been with the Comtesse for two days," Zela said, "but, except for that letter, which came this morning, there has been nothing that I could think of as being a clue of any kind or even a suggestion of one."

The Marquis was silent as if he was thinking of a course of action.

And then he asked Zela,

"Does the Comtesse have a safe where she places her jewels?"

Zela's eyes opened wide.

"I never thought of that!" she exclaimed. "I have been in her bedroom, but I did not see a safe, which is usually an ugly and ungainly piece of furniture."

"The Comtesse was wearing many jewels tonight," the Marquis said. "And last night she had on a stupendous diamond necklace."

"It belongs to Lord Grandon," Zela told him, "and he has only lent it to her and I am sure it's very unlucky because it originally belonged to Queen Marie Antoinette."

The Marquis gave an exclamation.

"I thought vaguely it had a history! Now, of course, I remember that Grandon has it in his superb collection."

"He lent it to the Comtesse to wear because she was going to Marlborough House," Zela informed him.

"She actually gave it back?" the Marquis remarked. "That is surprising."

Zela laughed.

"I think it would be too obvious and Lord Grandon would make too much of a fuss if she had stolen it!"

"What we are concerned with," the Marquis said, "is the money that you say she has taken from your father. Will you tell me how much it was?"

Zela hesitated for a brief moment.

Then she responded,

"I suppose it does not matter you knowing. It was fifty thousand pounds, my Lord."

The Marquis stared at her.

"As much as that! I am not at all surprised that you are so upset."

"We shall have to sell everything that is saleable in our – house," Zela related. "Even then I don't think that we shall be able to raise so much – "

She gave a little sob before she finished,

" – and what will happen to Papa and me?"

The Marquis's hand tightened on hers.

"I promise you," he said, "I will do everything in my power to save you and to save the two men who are in the same position as you. Heaven knows how many more there may be."

"What can we – do?" Zela asked him anxiously.

The Marquis looked out at the moonlight.

Zela could see his profile silhouetted against the clear sky and she thought how handsome and distinguished he was.

She felt certain that if anyone could save her father it was him.

There was something about the Marquis that was completely different to any man she had ever met before.

She knew that it was, in fact, the vibrations coming from him.

Not only from his hand, which was still holding on to hers but also from his whole being.

It was not surprising that he had done so much in India and he had been a hero who, as Dobson had said, deserved to be awarded the Victoria Cross for bravery in the face of the enemy.

She suddenly knew, as if someone was telling her, that the Marquis would save her father, just as he would save his friend and Mr. Steven Howe.

Without being aware of it her fingers now tightened on his.

He turned his head to look at her.

"We have to win," he asserted, "and with God's help we will."

"That is what I was thinking and I am so very very lucky that you are here, my Lord, and that you – will help me."

"Just as you have helped me. And now I will tell you what I want you to do."

He saw that Zela was listening with her eyes fixed on his.

"First," he said quietly, "it would be imperative to know where the Comtesse locks up her jewellery at night which, I am quite certain, will be in a safe of some sort. Do everything you can to find out where and what make of safe it is."

Zela nodded.

"Secondly," he continued, "because you and I have to save a number of others, bring me any letters like the one you have just given me from Steven Howe."

"Do you really think," Zela asked him, "that the Comtesse has told the same story – to every man she has taken money from."

She hesitated over the question because it seemed so unpleasant.

"The Comtesse has been in London long enough," the Marquis replied, "for there to be quite a number of men who are suffering at her hands. And, of course, we still have to prove that the Ruler she speaks about and who is supposedly dead, ever really existed."

"I think perhaps my father may do that," Zela said. "He has gone to Paris to find the man the Comtesse told him was dealing directly with the Eastern Ruler. His name is Monsieur Henri Monte."

The Marquis repeated the name and she knew that he would not forget it.

"Now," Zela suggested, "I think that I should go back to the Comtesse's house."

"Wait a moment," the Marquis said. "We have to arrange when we will meet again and also if you find the safe somewhere in the Comtesse's bedroom I want to know what make it is."

Zela looked at him in surprise.

"I have learned," he explained to her, "about quite a number of safes and that is something, if there is one, you and I can do together."

"But when," Zela asked, "and how?"

The Marquis smiled at her as if she was being a little stupid.

"Firstly what is the Comtesse doing tomorrow?" he asked.

Zela hesitated because for a brief moment she had forgotten.

"Very well," the Marquis said. "I will tell you what she is doing. She is having luncheon with Lord Grandon and she is going with him, because he is returning to the country the following day, to the Duchess of Devonshire's dinner party tomorrow evening."

Zela gave a little gasp.

"Yes – of course. That is indeed what she is doing and she must have told me so."

"She mentioned it to me tonight casually," he said. "Therefore, if there is anything to explore, you and I will explore it tomorrow evening."

"It will be exciting to do that," Zela replied.

"At what time," the Marquis asked, "is the whole house quiet and the servants are in their own beds?"

"They are not allowed to come into the front of the house after ten o'clock," Zela told him.

"Very well. So I will knock on the door as I did tonight at ten-thirty. But you must, before that, give me the name of the safe."

"If I find it, what shall I do?" Zela enquired.

"Put the name in an envelope and drop it through the letterbox of my front door," the Marquis replied. "You know where my house is just across the garden."

Zela nodded as she knew exactly where it was.

"I will try my best to do what you want," she said. "But, if I cannot find the safe, will you still come?"

"I will most definitely be with you at ten-thirty," the Marquis promised, "and thank you so much for being so helpful."

"I need to thank you, my Lord, and I am so very very grateful that you are being – so kind to me," Zela said.

She paused for a moment before she added,

"It has been very frightening working on my own."

"Of course it has," the Marquis agreed at once. "I think you are extremely brave and your father must be very proud of you."

He rose as he spoke and went outside the Temple.

"Now hurry home and go to bed," he urged. "It's no use lying awake worrying, leave that to me."

"Thank you, thank you," Zela enthused.

She looked up at him.

She was standing in the moonlight and the Marquis thought that it was quite impossible for any woman to look so lovely, so ethereal and so exquisite.

She was so unlike any other woman he had ever seen before.

He could not explain to himself why he thought that, but there was a distinct difference about Zela.

For a moment they stood gazing at each other.

Then with a little murmur Zela turned away and ran towards the gate.

She was sensible enough, the Marquis noticed, to wend her way through the trees.

If she had gone to the side of the garden, she might have been seen. Someone could have been looking out of one of the windows of No. 18.

He watched until he saw her slip through the gate and close it behind her.

Then she ran the short distance to the Comtesse's house and pushed open the door she had left unlocked.

Only then did she turn back and look to where she had left the Marquis, but it was impossible to see him as the trees were in the way.

She went in and shut the door, remembering not to bolt it.

So, as far as the household was concerned, the last person to leave the house would be the gentleman who had been with the Comtesse.

They would not say anything, yet they would think it strange if tomorrow morning they found that the door was bolted on the inside.

Zela hurried upstairs to her bedroom.

She undressed and before she climbed into bed she knelt down.

She was thanking God.

Thanking Him with a happiness that she had not felt since she had left home.

She felt strongly that somehow with the blessing of God everyone involved would be saved.

To her surprise Zela slept peacefully.

She had really wanted to think about the Marquis and how truly kind and supportive he was, but she was very tired.

She fell asleep almost as soon as her head touched the pillow.

*

She was woken by Hannah, who came in to call her rather than leave it to one of the housemaids.

"It's a nice day," she said, as she drew back the curtains, "and I'm hopin', Miss Lane, you'll 'ave a chance of getting' out in the fresh air today. It's not right that a girl of your age should be cooped up in 'ere seein' to all them endless letters."

"I have to go shopping in the afternoon," Zela said a little dolefully.

At the same time her heart was singing.

She was sure that the Marquis was thinking of her as she was thinking of him.

She had the usual pile of letters and invitations to attend to.

It was only when the Comtesse had left the house for a luncheon engagement with Lord Grandon that she had the opportunity she was waiting for.

She went along to the Comtesse's bedroom and, as she expected, Hannah was in there tidying up.

Hannah had just finished making the bed with one of the housemaids and the girl left the room as Zela came in.

"I just came to ask you," Zela said, "if you would give me the name of the lip salve that Madame uses. She told me that she has put it on the list she wants me to buy for her and I will get into trouble if it's not the make that she is using at the moment."

"You will indeed," Hannah agreed. "I'll go and find the pot so that you can take it with you."

"Thank you very much," Zela smiled at her.

She was looking carefully around the room as she spoke, but could see no sign of a safe.

Then she noticed that the lovely diamond earrings that the Comtesse had worn last night were lying on the dressing table.

"Those earrings are very pretty," she commented, "and I am sure that they are worth a great deal of money. Should you not put them somewhere safe?"

Hannah looked towards the earrings that she had obviously not seen before.

"That's very unlike Madame," she said, "she must 'ave been in an 'urry and forgot."

"They might be stolen if they are left lying about," Zela remarked.

"I'll see that doesn't 'appen," Hannah retorted.

"Do you have a safe here where you can put them?" Zela enquired.

Hannah gave a little laugh.

"There be a safe of sorts, but then I don't suppose Madame would trust me to open it. No, I'll 'ave to put these earrings in one of the drawers, cover them over with an 'andkerchief and 'ope if there be a burglar, 'e'll not find 'em."

Zela laughed.

"It sounds rather complicated. Where is the safe if there is one?"

125

"I'll give you three guesses," Hannah teased, "and I bet you a bar of chocolate you'll not get it right."

"Now you are being mysterious," Zela said. "Do tell me where it is."

"In that chest of drawers," Hannah replied.

She pointed to one at the other end of the room and it was a very pretty marquetry chest inlaid with mother-of-pearl.

Zela knew that it was quite old and valuable and what was somewhat unusual about it was that it had three clusters of flowers down the front of the three drawers and these had obviously been added at a later time to make it more ornamental.

"That's not a safe," Zela said aloud.

"That's where you lose your bet," Hannah giggled.

She walked across to the chest of drawers and then pulled the carved flowers away from the bottom drawer.

Ordinarily it was where the keyhole would be and Zela saw that there was indeed a large rather ugly keyhole.

It appeared far too modern to have been inserted there when the chest was built.

"That be Madame's safe," Hannah said. "I thinks meself there'll be a real to-do when she leaves and them that owns this 'ouse and the furniture sees just what she's done to that pretty chest."

Zela then knelt down on the floor to inspect it more carefully.

"It certainly looks very out of place," she remarked, "and spoils the beauty of the way that the mother-of-pearl has been inserted onto the drawers."

"That's what I thinks," Hannah said. "But, as soon as Madame arrives, she sends for a locksmith and 'as this done. It weren't my place to interfere, but I bet she 'as to pay a good sum for it when she leaves."

"I am sure she will," Zela agreed, "and it does seem a pity to have damaged it."

"Put the posy back where it comes from," Hannah said, throwing it down to her. "It's not our business, thank goodness."

She turned away to pick up the diamond earrings from the dressing table.

Then it was easy for Zela to look at the name on the safe.

It was rather difficult to see, but she thought that it was something like 'Sims'.

As she had never bothered with the names of safes before, it meant nothing to her.

Then, as Hannah put the diamond earrings away in the dressing table, they walked back to the housekeeper's room where luncheon was waiting for them.

*

Later that afternoon, when she had completed all the shopping that the Comtesse required, Zela walked back to Berkeley Square.

When she reached Buckwood House, she put the envelope she had just taken from her handbag addressed to the Marquis through the letterbox.

Hoping that no one had seen her, she hurried away to No. 18.

It seemed to her that the hours passed very slowly.

At a quarter to eight Lord Grandon arrived in his closed carriage to collect the Comtesse so that they could go together to the party at Devonshire House, which only a short distance away in Piccadilly.

"It would be absurd for me to take the carriage out to go such a short distance," Zela heard the Comtesse say to Dobson, "so his Lordship is fetching me. He will, of course, bring me back and don't forget to have a light in the hall and no one must wait up for me."

As this was a regular occurrence, Dobson merely said, "Yes, *madame*," and inclined his head.

The Comtesse certainly looked magnificent tonight.

She was dressed in a gown of emerald green with peacock feathers mixed with emeralds in her hair and she had an emerald necklace round her neck.

Although she hated her, Zela had to admit that she was very beautiful and, dressed in that fantastic manner, it would be impossible for anyone not to notice her.

Zela was, however, nervous that something might go wrong at the last moment.

The Comtesse then drove away in Lord Grandon's carriage.

Zela, watching them leave from the top floor, gave a sigh of relief.

There was to be a big luncheon party tomorrow and Hannah and Dobson talked of nothing else while they ate their supper.

Then Hannah said that she was going to bed and Dobson went up the stairs to join his wife before they too retired.

Zela walked slowly to her own bedroom.

Because she was about to see the Marquis again she was wearing the prettiest of her simple evening gowns.

It was the one she wore at home when she dined alone with her father.

Because she had always done so, she changed every night when she had supper in the housekeeper's room.

The gown she was wearing now was of a very soft muslin and it made her look even more ethereal than she had the previous night.

At precisely half past ten the Marquis came into the house, having knocked softly on the front door.

As Zela opened the door, he thought that she was even lovelier than she had been when they had met before.

Zela took him first into the little sitting room next to the front door.

Before she could speak the Marquis said,

"It was clever of you to find out the make of the safe."

"I think you ought to know that it is a very strange-looking safe," Zela remarked. "In fact the Comtesse had a special lock made on a beautiful antique inlaid chest which I am sure will annoy the person who actually owns it."

She noticed as she was speaking that the Marquis held a small case in his hand.

"I think," he suggested, "that we will work first and talk afterwards. If there is nothing in the safe, then we will have to think where we can look next."

"Yes, of course," Zela agreed. "I did not want you to be disappointed because it is not a proper safe."

He smiled at her as if she was being childish.

She walked ahead of him out of the sitting room and up the stairs.

Both of them knew that it would be a grave mistake to speak. Voices carried and it would be a disaster if one of the servants came to investigate who was moving about in the house.

Zela led the way into the Comtesse's bedroom and she was aware that the Marquis knew where it was.

But she did not want to think about that.

There were two oil lamps left burning by the bed for the Comtesse when she returned.

Also there was a little gold candelabrum with three candles on the dressing table.

Zela saw that the Marquis was now looking round the room with rather a perplexed expression on his face.

Having closed the door gently so that they could not be overheard, she said,

"You will not be able to guess where the safe is, my Lord."

"Then show me," he insisted.

Zela went to the chest of drawers and took off the little arrangement of carved flowers that hid the lock.

The Marquis looked at her and laughed.

"That is certainly original. I expected something quite different."

"Do you think – you can open it?" Zela asked him nervously.

The Marquis went down on his knees and opened his little case and she could see that it was filled with small instruments of every sort.

"It does seem wicked," he said "to have spoilt this valuable cabinet and I am afraid that what I have to do will not improve it."

Zela did not answer.

She just thought that, if after all this trouble, there was nothing at all inside the safe they would be frustrated and feel rather stupid.

And then they would find it very difficult to explain what had happened if the Comtesse suspected that they were the culprits.

It took the Marquis nearly ten minutes to remove the lock.

When it eventually came away, Zela, who had been watching him without speaking, gave a little cry,

"You have done it!"

The Marquis stood up and pulled his case and his instruments out of the way.

Then he took hold of the two handles, which were also beautifully inset with mother-of-pearl.

He pulled at the drawer.

For a second it seemed to resist him and Zela drew in her breath.

Then he pulled it open and she moved forward to look inside and, when she had done so, she gave a gasp and then a cry of joy.

Arranged in the bottom drawer of the locked chest there was everything that they had been looking for.

It only took three seconds to find what belonged to her father.

Everything was packaged in large envelopes.

Then, just as if the Comtesse would have difficulty remembering its contents, written on top of each one were the initials of the man she had taken money from.

Zela saw a large package with 'D.L.' on it.

She bent down and picked it up in her arms.

"This is all Papa's," she cried. "Oh, how could you have been – so clever. Oh, thank you, *thank you*!"

The Marquis saw one package marked with Charles Windell's initials and another with 'S.H.' on it that he knew was Mr. Steven Howe's.

There were, however, four other packages.

They were not quite as large as the one that Zela was holding, but larger than Charles Windell's.

On one side of the drawer there were two smaller velvet boxes that he guessed must contain the Comtesse's jewellery.

Then the Marquis saw at the end of the drawer that there was something different.

It was a flat round box and, as he looked at it, Zela followed the direction of his eyes.

She wondered why the box was so different to the other packages and then she remembered that she had seen it before.

It was the box that the Frenchman had put into the secretaire in the boudoir.

She had seen him doing it when she came to collect the Queen Marie Antoinette necklace and she remembered how he had looked round at her.

Then he had quickly pushed the box he was holding in his hand into the drawer.

There had been something decidedly suspicious in the way that he did it, although she had hardly noticed it at the time, as she was so intent on putting the necklace back outside the Comtesse's bedroom door.

Now a sudden thought struck her.

"I have just thought of something," she said aloud to the Marquis.

"What is it, Zela?" he asked her.

"I think," she went on, "although I might be wrong, that the round box there contains the real diamond necklace that belonged to Queen Marie Antoinette while the one that Lord Grandon has is a fake."

The Marquis stared at her.

Then bending down he picked up the box.

There was a piece of thin string tied over it which the Marquis broke.

Then when he raised the lid, Zela saw, as she had expected, the diamond necklace.

To her it was obviously the one that the Comtesse had worn when she went to the party with Lord Grandon.

"Are you saying," the Marquis asked her, "that this has been stolen from Lord Grandon?"

"Yes, it has been replaced by a French jeweller who completed making a copy of it the night that the Comtesse – wore it."

Zela stopped for breath and then went on,

"She told me it needed a little repair. But I think when she borrowed it for the first time the French jeweller made a copy. He completed it the other evening and he was working on it in the boudoir for an hour before I let him out of the house."

"I did actually see him leaving," the Marquis said. "And I thought at first that he was a burglar. He certainly looked a rather strange person to be leaving so late."

"We must get the necklace back to Lord Grandon," Zela insisted. "I am sure that it would upset him greatly to lose it."

"He will have it back, so will all the other owners of this extraordinary collection in front of us," the Marquis asserted.

He looked round as he spoke.

By the dressing table there was a pretty but fairly large wastepaper basket.

He fetched it and started putting into it everything that was in the drawer.

Zela watched him intently, holding tightly onto her father's package in her arms.

The wastepaper basket was full to the brim by the time the Marquis had put everything into it except for the Comtesse's jewels.

The box containing the necklace was on the top.

Then the Marquis closed the drawer and placed the carved arrangement of flowers back in the front to hide the broken lock.

He picked up the wastepaper basket and his case.

"The sooner I take this to safety the better," he said.

"Yes, of course," Zela agreed.

The Marquis went down the stairs first and, when he reached the front door, he put down the wastepaper basket to open the door.

Zela had followed him and she was still holding the precious bundle of her father's banknotes in her arms.

She put it down on the last step, meaning to help him, and then the Marquis turned to look at her.

"We are going to make a number of people very happy tomorrow," he said. "Go upstairs now and pack up your case and I will collect you as soon as you have had breakfast and drive you home."

"I cannot believe that this is really happening," Zela sighed. "You have been wonderful, absolutely wonderful, and, as you say, so many people will be happy who have been in the depths of despair at losing so much money"

"We have won our battle," the Marquis said. "And, if I have done well, so have you. I cannot imagine any other woman would have been so brave or have helped me so cleverly without making any fuss."

Zela raised her head to look at him.

"You saved my Papa," she said, "and that is what matters to me. Thank you, thank you from the bottom of my heart."

The way she spoke was very moving and then the Marquis saw that there were tears in her eyes.

He bent forward and put his arms round her.

He kissed her intending it to be a kindly gentle kiss on her cheek.

Then somehow his lips touched hers and a sublime ecstasy shot through him.

It was different to anything he had ever felt before and he could not explain it even to himself.

He only knew that this kiss was different and unlike any kiss he had ever known.

His lips became more possessive.

He held Zela even closer to him so that her body seemed to melt into his.

Then he suddenly remembered just what was lying beside him and set her free.

"Nine o'clock tomorrow morning," he murmured, "and I will not be late."

His voice sounded strange even to himself.

He then picked up the wastepaper basket and his tool case and went out through the door.

Automatically, as if she was in a dream, Zela closed it.

She ran up the stairs holding her precious bundle of banknotes against her breasts.

When she reached her bedroom, she put it down on the bed.

Just in case, by some terrible mistake it did not contain what she expected, she opened up the end of the parcel.

She saw that there were plenty of notes of a high denomination and she did not have to look any closer.

'How could he have been so wonderful? How could he possibly have done this for Papa and those other people who the Comtesse had crooked?' she asked herself.

Then she remembered that the Marquis was coming for her tomorrow morning and she had to pack.

She found her suitcase and then put the precious banknotes at the bottom of it.

Next she began to take down her dresses from the wardrobe and then laid them in the case one after another.

There was not really much to pack as she had only brought enough for a week or two.

She took off the gown that she was wearing and put it on top.

Then suddenly, when she should have taken off her clothes and put on her nightgown, she had an idea.

Why should her father be involved in the row that would surely happen tomorrow?

She had not told the Marquis her real name and there was no reason for him to know what it was.

However secret he might want to keep what had occurred, undoubtedly the servants would talk as she knew only too well.

And sooner or later the gossips of London would be relating just how very fortunate her father was to have his money back.

He would then be branded as one of the Comtesse's lovers, as would all the other men she had been involved with.

'I could not bear it,' Zela thought.

She carefully worked out in her mind exactly how she could avoid either her father being involved or herself.

She quickly put on the plain dress she had arrived in and found the hat that went with it.

Then she finished packing her case.

By this time it was still dark, but the dawn was not far away.

One thing was vitally important.

That she should leave the house before five o'clock.

If there was a great deal of work to do, Dobson, the housemaids and those who were helping in the kitchen would start work at five.

Zela went to the window and looked out.

The moon was waning and the stars were beginning to fade and it was only a question of time before the first light of dawn would appear in the East.

She could just see the roof of the little Temple in the garden of the Square.

Zela picked up her case and went very quietly down the stairs.

She let herself out of the front door.

At this time of the morning it would be difficult to find a Hackney carriage and so she would have to walk to Victoria Station.

As she was used to walking, it would not take her very long and she would not find it as arduous as any other woman might have done.

She went out into Berkeley Square.

She thought that the Marquis would be sleeping peacefully in his house on the other side of it.

She said a silent goodbye to him in her heart.

And she would never see him again, but she hoped that some time he would think of her.

She knew that it would be impossible, absolutely impossible, for her ever to forget his kiss.

CHAPTER SEVEN

Zela found that she had quite a long wait when she reached Victoria Station.

Fortunately the waiting room was open and so she sat comfortably in it.

There was an early morning train picking up milk and produce and it stopped at every Station.

She paid for her ticket and found a 'Ladies Only' carriage that remained empty all the way.

It was well after seven o'clock when she finally arrived at Canterbury Station.

Zela thought it would be difficult to find a Hackney carriage at that time in the morning.

Luckily there was a young farmer she knew who had brought some produce to be sent by train and he said at once that he would be delighted to give her a lift home in his rather battered cart.

If she had found a carriage for hire, she would have gone straight to the bank. Her father's main bank was in London, but there was a subsidiary in Canterbury.

This was impossible for her as the young farmer was very anxious to return to his home.

Zela therefore decided that she would go in later in the afternoon and Armstrong could drive her.

She did, however, persuade the farmer to stop at the first Post Office they passed.

She sent a telegram to her father at the Travellers Club in Paris saying,

"*Have found what you lost, Papa. Come home*! *Much love, Zela.*"

As she climbed back into the farmer's cart, she felt as if a great weight had been taken off her shoulders.

Now her father would no longer need to worry and things would soon be back to how they had been before.

When she arrived at Langdale Hall, she thanked the farmer profusely. And he said gallantly that it was a great privilege to have her on his cart.

As she walked in through the door, Brunt appeared and looked at her in astonishment.

"You're back, my Lady!" he exclaimed.

"Yes, I am back," Zela replied, "and I hope that everything is all right here."

"We have missed you, my Lady," Brunt said, "and there's a letter from his Lordship which came yesterday. I wondered what I should do about it."

"At least I have saved you having to send it on to me," Zela replied. "I would love some breakfast just as soon as Mrs. Brunt can manage it."

Brunt hurried away to the kitchen and Zela went into the study as she knew that Brunt would have put her father's letter on the writing desk.

She picked it up eagerly.

At the same time she was hoping that he had not been too unhappy these past days and now he could come home.

She opened the letter and read,

"*Dearest Zela,*

You will see that I have changed my address. But I will still come to the Travellers Club every day in case you have written to me there.

I am still searching for Monsieur Henri Monte, who has never been heard of at the address that the Comtesse gave me. I am beginning to think that he does not actually exist.

I have, however, just by chance found a very old friend here in Paris and that is Lady Sutton.

I think that you will remember her as she and her husband came to stay with us about two years ago.

He has now died and, as he was in the Diplomatic Service for so long in Paris, she decided to stay on here because she felt that she knew no one in England.

She has a truly magnificent house near the Champs Élysées and needless to say I am very comfortable.

She has now persuaded me to stay with her and has been very kind and understanding to me over the position we are in.

It will be very exciting and a wonderful opportunity for me and we are at the moment talking about our future.

I know, dearest Zela, you will love Edith Sutton when you get to know her.

Hoping to hear from you and I will write again in a day or so.

Much love from your very affectionate father."

Zela read the letter carefully a second time.

Then she knew without being told that her father would marry Lady Sutton.

She could remember her quite well. She was a very attractive woman who was married to a man who was quite a lot older than herself.

Lady Sutton could only be around thirty-seven or thirty-eight and it passed through Zela's mind that, if she did marry her father, she would be able to give him the son he had always wanted.

She was certain that her father would never love anyone as much as he had loved her beloved mother, yet Edith Sutton would make him a charming and affectionate wife.

What was more Zela remembered that Lord Sutton had been very rich.

'She will certainly prevent Papa from being lonely,' she thought, 'and having to struggle so much to keep the house and the stables going.'

Then, almost as if the words were scorched in front of her, she asked,

'But what about me?'

Of course she could stay at home as she always had and be content with riding the horses.

But her father's wife would be the Mistress in the house and, however kind they were to her, they would be happier if they were on their own.

Looking into the future, Zela was sure, as her father had said so often, that he would want her to have a Season in London.

She was a little old to come out as a *debutante*, yet there would be endless parties, luncheons, Receptions and many exciting things to do in London.

Perhaps if there was plenty of money she would be able to ride in Rotten Row.

But it would mean that they would expect her to get married as soon as someone her father approved of asked for her hand.

She felt her whole being revolt against the idea.

'I have no wish to be married,' she thought almost angrily.

Then she knew that it was not true.

The incredibly intense feelings when the Marquis had kissed her seemed to sweep over her again.

It was so wonderful, so perfect and so sublime.

She felt as if he had carried her up into the sky and her whole being had reached out towards him.

And, as he had drawn her closer, she felt as if their bodies melted into each other.

She put down her father's letter with a sigh.

'This is love,' she mused, 'and it is something very very glorious that I will never know again.'

She went into her bedroom to change into one of the cotton dresses she wore every day.

One of the women who came in from the village to help clean the house said 'good morning' to her.

Otherwise there was no one around and the house seemed very large and empty.

'I will go to the stables,' Zela told herself.

There was no need to wear riding clothes and when she was alone she rode just as she was. If the day was hot it was easier to wear a thin cotton dress than a heavy riding skirt.

Armstrong was pleased to see her.

"Ah, you're back, my Lady," he said. "We missed you when you was away."

"I am delighted to be back," Zela replied.

That was not exactly true.

But she was extremely glad to be away from No. 18 Berkeley Square.

But it was impossible for her not to think about the Marquis and how kind he had been to her.

She decided to go riding in the woods, which was an exercise she always enjoyed.

Yet today she did not see any of the rabbits and the squirrels that usually enchanted her.

She could only see the Marquis's handsome face and hear the deep tone of his voice.

'I have to forget him,' she told herself. 'If nothing else, he is the reason why I can never go back to London.'

She knew that if she went back to please her father as a *debutante* she would be nervous at every party just in case the Marquis was a guest.

If he was, then her heart would turn a somersault and it would be sheer agony to see him dancing perhaps with someone as beautiful as the Comtesse.

'It's finished. It's over,' she tried to tell herself.

When she trotted back into the stables, Armstrong asked her,

"Have you enjoyed your ride, my Lady?"

"It was splendid," Zela replied, but that was not the truth.

She had been daydreaming about the Marquis.

She was longing for him and had hardly been aware of what she was doing or where she was going.

'I have to forget him,' she told herself again and again.

The day drew on.

It was impossible to concentrate on all the things that she had always found so interesting in the past.

'How can I be so foolish?' she asked herself. 'I have fallen in love with a man, who now he has what he wants will never give me another thought.'

She wondered what he had said to the Comtesse and if Lord Grandon was astonished to find that his famous necklace had been copied and that he might have lost the original.

She kept imagining how happy both Steven Howe and Charles Windell must be, as by this time the Marquis would have given them back their money.

She had tea at half past four by herself in the study.

She was thinking it very likely that by this time her father would have received her telegram.

It would sweep away his depression and yet she doubted now whether he would come home immediately as she had expected him to do.

He would now have Lady Sutton to share in his excitement and perhaps they would celebrate by going out to dinner at some fashionable French restaurant.

'I am just here alone all by myself,' Zela thought miserably.

She rose from the tea table and walked over to the window.

Outside the sun was still shining on the flowers in the garden and the birds would soon be going to roost in the oak trees.

'At least all this will not be taken from us now,' she thought.

She knew that it was the idea of losing their home that had upset her father so much.

'It's ours! It's still ours!' she tried to say to herself triumphantly.

Yet somehow there was not the same elation that she would have felt a few days ago.

Instead of seeing the shadows gradually growing a little longer beneath the trees that she had loved since she was a child, all she could see was the Marquis's handsome face and his blue eyes gazing down at hers.

'I am trying to understand,' Zela scolded herself angrily, 'that I will never see him again and the sooner I forget all about him the better.'

Then, as she knew deep in her heart that the answer to that was an impossibility, she heard the door of the study open and Brunt entered.

"The Marquis of Buckwood, my Lady."

For a moment Zela felt as if she had been turned to stone.

Then, as she turned round slowly, she found that the Marquis had crossed the room.

He was standing quite near her.

She gazed at him and then, as her eyes met his, she managed to say a little incoherently,

"What has happened? What has gone wrong? Why are you – here?"

The words seemed to tumble out of her mouth, not even making sense.

The Marquis came a little nearer.

"I will answer all those questions in time," he said. "But for the moment I have one most important question to ask *you*."

Because he was so close to her, Zela felt herself tremble and she managed to ask in a very small voice,

"What is – it?"

"I want to know," the Marquis said, "what you felt when I kissed you?"

Zela's eyes opened wide.

Then, as she met his eyes, he saw an inexpressible rapture fill them.

Colour came into her cheeks and she looked away because she was suddenly feeling shy.

"Tell me," the Marquis urged her very quietly.

Zela knew that she had to obey him and in a voice that he could hardly hear she answered,

"I felt as if I – touched the stars."

The Marquis made a sound that was almost a cry of triumph.

Then his arms were round her and he pulled her close to him.

"That is exactly what I felt too," he sighed, "and I could hardly believe that it was true."

Then his lips were on hers.

He was kissing her gently at first.

Then, as he felt the incredibly marvellous sensation he had before, his kiss became more possessive and more compelling.

To Zela it was as if the Heavens opened.

She was not only touching the stars.

They were in her breast, in her heart and on her lips.

The Marquis kissed her and went on kissing her as if they were both floating up into the sky.

The Gates of Heaven were opening and a celestial choir of angels was singing.

It seemed a long time later that the Marquis raised his head and breathed,

"My darling, my sweet, how can you make me feel like this? I have never before known anything so perfect or so wonderful."

"I love – you," Zela whispered.

"I love you and I thought that I would never see you again," the Marquis said. "How could you have done anything so utterly cruel and wicked as to run away like that without telling me where you were going."

"I did not think – you would want to see me again after I had found – what you wanted."

"That was one thing, but what we are to each other is something very different," the Marquis said. "I knew when I kissed you that you are what I have been looking for and seeking all my life, but was quite certain did not exist."

His lips touched hers again before he went on,

"This is love, my darling one. The real love that I thought only existed in books or in my imagination."

Zela thought that this could not be happening to her and that she must be dreaming.

"I know now that I have never been in love before," the Marquis was saying. "You are mine, my darling, and now that I have found you I will never let you go."

"It cannot – be true," Zela said a little brokenly.

"It is true," he answered, "and, when I found that you had gone, I thought that I would go mad."

"But how did you find me? No one knew who I was."

"You are underrating my ability," he replied with a smile. "I knew that you had not given me your real name, but your father's initials were written on the money he had given the Comtesse and, of course, Dobson told me your father's name and that he had been with the Comtesse."

"I never – thought of that," Zela murmured.

"Dobson has also told me the other people whose names were on the packages and I have arranged for them all to be notified that their money is intact. As I don't know them, they have no idea who their benefactor is."

She was listening intently and the Marquis went on,

"You told me that your father was in Paris and I suppose we can let him know that his money is now safe. But what is more important is that I have now found *you*."

He did not wait for her to answer, but was kissing her again.

He was kissing her passionately until she felt that once again she was flying into the sky and the stars were glittering within her breasts.

Very much later the Marquis said,

"Tell me, my beautiful one, how soon can we be married?"

Zela gave a little gasp and then she hid her face against his neck.

"I love you," she whispered. "I love you and you fill my whole world, but how can I possibly make you happy?"

She gave a sigh and went on,

"You are so brave and wonderful and have done so many marvellous things that I am afraid you will soon be bored with me."

The Marquis pulled her a little closer and laughed.

It was a very gentle sound.

"I have told you, my precious," he said, "I have never, in my whole life, felt for a woman what I feel for you. Although I was determined not to get married, what I really meant was that I would not get married until I found you."

"But if we are married and I disappoint you," Zela said, "then all I will want to do is to die."

"You are not going to die, Zela. We are going to be wildly and madly happy because we have so much to do together and I cannot do it without you."

She did not respond, so he put his fingers under her chin and turned her face up to his.

"You are more beautiful than any woman I have ever seen," he said in a deep voice. "But our love is much more than that. I love you because your heart beats with my heart. And my soul, which I have never worried about before, is, I know, the other half of your soul."

He kissed her forehead before continuing,

"We are one kind of person, my precious, and I cannot live without you any more than I could live without my arms and my feet."

Zela gave a little cry.

"It's so wonderful," she whispered, "I know that I am not really hearing this and I have somehow gone to Heaven without my being aware of it."

"That is just how it will be when we are married," the Marquis said. "And I want to know how soon that is possible?"

Zela put her two hands on his chest to push him a little way from her.

"You are going too fast," she said. "Tell me what happened and how you managed to come here so quickly."

The Marquis did not speak and after a moment she asked in a very low voice,

"What did you say to the Comtesse?"

"Nothing," the Marquis replied.

"Nothing," she repeated.

"I rose very early," he explained. "And – "

He stopped.

"We cannot just stand here while I tell you what has happened," he said. "Sit down, but stay very close, my darling, because I am so frightened that you will disappear again and I will have to go all round the world searching for you."

Zela gave a little laugh.

"I am here and I promise I will not run away."

"I was very angry with you for doing anything that would have made me frantic if Dobson had not known who your father is."

"You were telling me about the Comtesse."

"What I was telling you," the Marquis said, "was that my first thought when I woke up very early was to put my friend, Charles, out of his agony. I went to his flat, where I knew he would be and, when I gave him back the money he had given to the Comtesse, he could not believe that it was true."

"I can understand him feeling like that," Zela said.

"The same thing happened when I reached Steven Howe. By that time, having had no breakfast, I called on Lord Grandon who was staying at the Ritz."

"What did he say?" Zela asked.

"When I informed him that his necklace had been copied, he nearly had a stroke. But he was exceedingly grateful, as you might well imagine, to receive the genuine necklace back that you and I had found in that weird safe."

"So what did you do then?" Zela enquired.

"As I did not know the names of the other people on the packets, I was determined to make the Comtesse tell me who they were."

"And did she?"

"When I arrived at No. 18 Berkeley Square," the Marquis said, "she had already left."

"Gone!" Zela exclaimed. "But where had she gone to?"

"She had gone from the house by six o'clock in the morning. So, soon after Lord Grandon had left her, she must have been putting away in the safe the diamonds that she was wearing when she dined with him."

"And then she found it empty," Zela added almost beneath her breath.

"I gather it must have been a shock because, when she roused the household, she made everyone start packing up her things. And by everyone I mean all those working in the kitchen as well as all the maids and Dobson."

"And she left?"

150

"They told me," the Marquis replied, "that they had never worked so quickly in the whole of their lives. The Comtesse had left before six o'clock taking everything she possessed with her."

"Where has she gone?" Zela wondered.

The Marquis made a gesture with his hands.

"Does it matter? But I can tell you one thing, that neither London nor Paris will ever see her again. Although there will be a lot of curiosity, there will be no scandal."

"I can only thank God for that. I was so worried that Papa would be involved."

"No one but you and I will have the slightest idea that he had been crooked by a very clever, unscrupulous and beautiful woman."

"Just how could she behave like that when she is so beautiful?" Zela asked.

"She betrayed her beauty," the Marquis said. "As my Nanny used to say to me, and I am sure your Nanny said the same, 'beauty is only skin deep'. She was betrayed by her own greed for more and more money and she had no compunction about who she ruined on the way so long as she ended up with what she wanted."

Zela laughed.

"What I want," the Marquis added, "is your beauty, my darling, because it is not just your exquisite and lovely face that attracts me but the beauty of your thoughts, your mind, your heart and again I have to say it – your soul."

"How can you say such wonderful things to me?" Zela sighed. "You are just so brave and so marvellous and everyone thinks that you deserve the Victoria Cross."

"I have something much more important and much more valuable," the Marquis answered, "and that is you, my darling Zela."

He pulled her closer into his arms.

When he tried to kiss her, she put her fingers on his lips to prevent him.

"Can I really – marry you?" Zela asked him a little hesitantly.

"I am going to marry you," the Marquis insisted, "as soon as it is possible. In fact I am not waiting for your father or anyone else."

"Suppose you regret later being too hasty?"

"I have told you that is impossible," he replied. "I have always believed that quite a number of women have wanted to marry me for one reason or another and you are not being very complimentary!"

"It is only because I love you so much that I could not bear you to be disappointed or to wish later that you had thought again more carefully," Zela said.

She paused for a moment before she went on,

"I do love you with all my heart and soul and I will do everything possible to make you happy. But – "

"There are no buts," the Marquis interrupted. "I am already the happiest man in the world because I know that you are mine and I have found you after what now seems a long and dreary search."

Then he was kissing Zela again, kissing her even more demandingly than he had kissed her before.

He only stopped when she put up her hands as if in protest.

"Am I frightening you, my darling?" he asked. "I hope not, but it's just that you excite me so wildly I find it very difficult to control myself."

"I am not frightened," Zela replied. "Except that I realise how little I know about love. Will you promise to teach me to love you as you want to be loved so that I can always make you happy?"

The Marquis held her close.

He thought of the women who had passed through his life at one time or another and how unimportant they seemed to him now.

He told himself that he must be extremely gentle and understanding with Zela as she was so young, so pure and so innocent.

At the same time he knew that he was right when he said that he had found the one woman in the world who was the other half of himself.

It would be impossible for them not to be blissfully happy for the rest of their lives.

He gazed down into Zela's eyes.

"I love you, my beautiful one," he said. "Together we will make our love the perfection it was meant to be and by being so happy ourselves we will make everyone else we come into contact with happy too."

He remembered as he spoke that it was something he wanted to do as a boy and now he knew that, with Zela to help him, they would both be loved by all those they employed and all those who worked and lived on the land he owned.

He would keep away from them and from her all the enemies of misery, unhappiness and poverty.

And these were just as terrifying and cruel as the Russians were in India.

To protect those he loved, whether it was a country or a person, he knew that he had to believe not only in his own abilities but also that he was guided and helped by God.

Already he and Zela had not only found that it was the truth that they had been blessed by the Divine in that they had come together in the most unlikely way.

As if Zela knew instinctively what the Marquis was thinking, she sighed,

"I love you and adore you, Rupert. And, whatever happens and however difficult life will be, our love will keep us together for ever."

"You can be quite sure of that," he answered her. "And, my precious, our love will increase as the years go past, so we must teach our children to search as we have searched for the real love that God has graciously given us."

As he said the last words, his lips were on Zela's.

He kissed her and once again they were flying up to the sky and touching the stars one by one.

Then there was only LOVE LOVE LOVE.

Manufactured by Amazon.ca
Bolton, ON